Who Took Henry and Mr. Z?

Who Took
Henry and Mr. Z?

Dave Glaze

Coteau Books

Edited by Dave Margoshes.
Cover painting by Janet Wilson.
Cover and book design by Ruth Linka.
Typeset by Ruth Linka.
Printed and bound in Canada.

The publisher gratefully acknowledges the financial assistance of the Saskatchewan Arts Board, the Canada Council, the Department of Canadian Heritage, and the City of Regina Arts Commission.

Canadian Cataloguing in Publication Data
Glaze, Dave, 1947-
    Who took Henry and Mr. Z?
    ISBN 1-55050-107-0

I. Title.
PS8563.L386W46 1996   jC813'.54   C96-920060-9
PZ7.G42Wh 1996

COTEAU BOOKS
401-2206 Dewdney Avenue
Regina, Saskatchewan
S4R 1H3

For my mother and father.

Intruder: *someone who goes where they're not supposed to be. Usually doing something they're not supposed to be doing.*

Definition by Winston.

MONDAY

Chapter 1

WITH HIS SHARP FRONT TEETH, HENRY nicked tiny slices from a piece of apple. He held the apple away from him and chewed the mush in his mouth. Checking to one side and then the other, he sniffed for any new scents in the air.

Close by, Mr. Z lay snoozing. His head and front paws rested inside the end of a cardboard tube. Not one hair on Mr. Z's fat, furry body had moved since he'd finished his meal of dry pellets and water.

Both guinea pigs had thick, shiny coats. Henry's long hair was the colour of butterscotch. On Mr. Z's back, the short creamy-white hair was sprinkled with dark brown dots and streaks that made the shape of the letter Z.

The two pets lived at the back of Mrs. Whitestar's grade five classroom. Their home was a handmade table – a piece of plywood that stood on four wooden legs about the height of the nearby desks. Along the edges of the table, narrow strips of wood stood up to pen them in. A water bottle was wired to one side. Lining the floor of their home were layers of newspaper covered with a coating of wood chips and sawdust. Near the cardboard tube and food dish was a shoe box with a hole cut in the end.

Around the room, children sat hunched over their math books or lay, heads together, in twos and threes on the floor. Winston and Caroline, their desks pushed side by side, were sharing Caroline's textbook.

"It's easy to tell who's smarter," Winston said.

"What?" Caroline asked. "Who?"

"Mr. Z," Winston said. "Just look at him. He doesn't waste any time running around the cage. He just lies there, thinking."

"Guinea pigs don't think." Caroline copied out another question. Flecks of colour sparkled along her glasses as her head shifted from textbook to notebook.

"You don't know that," Winston said. "It looks like he's relaxing, but he could be dreaming up some plan to escape or something." Winston patted the side of his head. Then he licked the tips of his fingers and tried to make his hair lie flat. No matter how often he brushed it, a little clump of hair always seemed to be sticking out from his head.

"Why would he want to escape?" Caroline asked. "He's got everything he could ever want right where he is. And guinea pigs can't climb, remember? He'd never get over the side."

"He might. He could butt the box over to the edge, with his snout, right? And then sort of get on top of the box. And then...."

"Forget it!" Caroline flipped to a back page to check an answer. "I want to finish this. I don't want homework tonight."

"No, but if a desk had been left beside their cage, then he could sort of slide over the edge...."

"Good morning, girls and boys." A man's loud voice startled the children.

Mr. Kroop, the vice-principal, strode through the open door to Mrs. Whitestar's desk. As the children looked his way, he pulled on the end of his tie while jerking the knot sharply left, right, then left again. From neck to balding forehead, his skin flushed a deep shade of red. Mr. Kroop hooked his thumbs over the top of his pants. As he thrust back his shoulders, his stomach seemed to bulge out toward the students.

"So nice to see everyone working," he said. "I know how you hate to be disturbed." He chortled at his joke.

"I just want to remind you," he went on, "that our principal, Mrs. Bobowski, won't be here for the next three days. She'll be at a convention. And that means," Mr. Kroop tipped onto his toes,

WHO TOOK HENRY AND MR. Z?

pushing his stomach further over his belt, "that I will be in charge."

Rolling back on his heels, Mr. Kroop rubbed his hands together. "I'm sure the school will run smoothly during that time. But, if there are problems, you should come to me. And I will sort them out." Mr. Kroop smiled again. "Now carry on with what you were doing."

Mr. Kroop turned to leave, then looked back at Mrs. Whitestar. The ends of his lips had twisted down like a clown's sad mouth. "If you must have those animals, you could at least keep the cage clean," he said. "The smell is bad for anyone trying to learn."

Mrs. Whitestar sniffed twice, then shrugged. "It's not so bad," she said. "Tomorrow's the day we usually change the bedding."

When the vice-principal had gone, Mrs. Whitestar got up from her desk. She pulled her long black hair together at the back of her neck, then let it fall around her shoulders. "Keep doing your math," she said. "I'll be coming around to check on you."

Two children reached the guinea pig table as Mrs. Whitestar finished speaking. Fingers pinched the skin on the back of Mr. Z's neck.

"Donny!" Melissa scolded, "don't pick him up like that, you'll hurt him."

"This doesn't hurt him," Donny said, bringing Mr. Z's face close to his own. "He likes it."

"How would you like to be yanked up like that?" Melissa asked. She reached across the table to try and snatch the guinea pig.

"How would you like to shut up?" was Donny's answer. He twisted away from Melissa and cradled Mr. Z against his chest. Donny's sweat shirt, like the gym pants he wore every day, was soft and faded.

"Please share the guinea pigs," Mrs. Whitestar said from the front of the room.

"He was holding him wrong," Melissa whined.

"He's doing it right now," Mrs. Whitestar said. "You can take Henry for awhile, if you like."

When his teacher turned back to the student she was helping, Donny leaned over toward Melissa. He crossed his eyes and stuck a finger in his open mouth.

"Snake face," Melissa hissed as Donny returned to his desk. "You probably don't even have your work done."

Flicking her long blonde hair over her shoulder, Melissa scooped her left hand under Henry and held him just above the table. As he lay still in her palm, Melissa gently brushed sawdust from his fur. She spread her right hand over his body and tucked the guinea pig under her chin, then walked to her friend Kristie's desk. The two girls, their noses almost touching Henry's snout, cooed to the guinea pig.

"Do you want him?" Donny asked as he passed Winston's desk.

"Sure." Winston took Mr. Z in his hands and laid him on his lap. Resting his forehead on the top of his desk, he whispered to the guinea pig. Mr. Z crawled into the desk. A few moments later, Winston nudged Caroline with his elbow. "Now, watch this," he said.

"Okay, Mr. Z, on the count of three, come out of the desk. One ... two ... three." Winston sat back.

Caroline glanced over in time to see Mr. Z peer out and test the air.

"Hah! See!" Winston beamed. "Mr. Z is *astute. Clever. Knows when to do something.*"

"Yeah, right. He's probably hungry again."

"So, there's nothing wrong with that, is there Mr. Z?" With his fingertips, Winston caressed the top of the guinea pig's head.

Winston coaxed the animal back onto his hand. He carried Mr. Z to the cage, and put the guinea pig down beside a leaf of lettuce. Mr. Z clutched the food between his paws, then started to nibble.

Where would you go if you ever did get out? Winston wondered. He ruffled the hair on the guinea pig's back, then smoothed it down again. He had no way of knowing that the next day he would be asking that question for real.

TUESDAY

Chapter 2

A S HE DID EVERY MORNING AT SEVEN O'CLOCK, Mr. Janzen unlocked the outside doors to the school. Before stepping inside, the janitor inhaled deeply the cool October air. Then he headed to his basement office to boil water for coffee.

A short time later, an intruder entered the school. In the silence of the empty building, running shoes squeaked a steady beat up a flight of stairs.

The intruder walked down the unlit second floor hall. On the right-hand side, from four open classroom doors, weak sunlight cut into the gloom. Veering left into a shadowy opening, the intruder pulled the door shut.

A few steps brought the intruder to Mrs. Whitestar's desk. A nylon backpack crackled to the floor. The intruder sat down in the teacher's chair and pulled a yellow plastic bag from the pack.

One hand braced against the desk as the other pulled at the wide top drawer. When it was completely open, both hands picked through the pencils, rulers, notebooks, and loose papers inside. Then the drawer was pushed back.

The top drawer on the right side of the desk was opened. A hand flicked aside scissors and felt pens, boxes of pins and thumbtacks, a hair-brush. That drawer was closed. A steady pull opened the heavy bottom drawer. The front held file folders. Behind the folders was an open space. A hand reached into the back and returned with fingers curled over an old-fashioned metal cookie tin. As the intruder turned the tin right side up, coins clinked onto the bottom.

The intruder tugged against the ridge that ran around the tin's lid. The container wouldn't open. From a pocket, the intruder pulled a silvery metal cigarette lighter about the size and shape of a roll of candies. When the lighter was pried against the top of the tin, the lid popped open. A pile of paper money sprang out like a jack-in-the-box. Bills slid out of the tin, over the intruder's lap, and onto the floor.

As the thief scooped the money from the tin, the lighter fell to the floor and rolled further under the desk. The handfuls of bills were shoved to the bottom of the plastic bag. By leaning sideways, the intruder could reach the few bills that had fallen near the legs of the chair. Loonies and quarters were poured from the tin into the bag. The intruder knotted the top of the bag and put it in the pack.

The lid was replaced and the tin put back in the desk. The bottom drawer squealed as it was closed. Motionless, the intruder listened for any movement in the hall.

Outside the windows, the sky was lightening. Glancing at the clock, the thief grabbed the pack and walked to the guinea pigs' table.

Henry lay with his snout pressed into a corner. He was lifted up by the back of the neck, then lowered rump first into the pack. Mr. Z never stirred while he was yanked from the table and dropped beside Henry.

The intruder pulled another plastic bag from a pocket of the pack. Using the shoebox as a shovel, some of the soiled shavings and guinea pig droppings were pushed into the plastic bag. The bag was laid on top of the guinea pigs.

The thief closed up the pack, walked swiftly to the door, listened for a few seconds, then left the room.

Chapter 3

ONE HOUR AFTER THE INTRUDER LEFT, Winston ambled along the hallway toward his locker. As he passed the door to his room, Winston saw Mrs. Whitestar working at her desk. He let his backpack fall to the floor, then opened his locker a crack. Bending down, he used his arm and leg to hold back a pile of books, loose papers and computer disks, sweaters, shoes, and plastic bags. He shared the space with Caroline, but all of this stuff was his. Caroline kept her gym shoes on the top shelf.

"Good morning, Winston." Mrs. Whitestar was standing in the classroom doorway.

"Oh, hi," he said. As he straightened up to smile at his teacher, Winston pushed down the tuft of hair on the side of his head.

"You're not supposed to be up here yet, you know," Mrs. Whitestar said.

"Well, I thought I'd better come up a bit early to see if my math book was here, because when I was going to do my homework last night I didn't have it. And if it's in here I could maybe still get my homework finished. At least some of it. And then—"

"No, no." Mrs. Whitestar held out her open hand to stop Winston. "I don't have time for a long explanation. I don't know how you sneaked by Mr. Kroop at the door, but I suppose if you're here you can stay." Mrs. Whitestar turned the page of the book she was reading.

For the next few minutes Winston poked at the things in his locker. Moments after the bell rang, the hall was filled with children. Mrs. Whitestar tucked her book under her arm and greeted each of her children as they arrived. Now that it was nine o'clock, Winston felt no rush to go into the classroom. Maybe, he thought, he'd wait where he was for Caroline. She was usually a few minutes late.

Melissa hurried out of the classroom and tugged on Mrs. Whitestar's sleeve. "You've got to come," she demanded. As she twisted to look behind her and then back to Mrs. Whitestar, Melissa's hair flew out to one side of her head and then the other. When Mrs. Whitestar pulled her arm from the girl's grip, Melissa crumpled her face as if in pain. "Something terrible has happened to Henry and Mr. Z," she cried. "They're gone!"

11

"Oh, they're probably just hiding in the shoe box again," Mrs. Whitestar said. She put a hand on Melissa's shoulder. "Let's go look. You, too, Winston," she said. "It's time to get started."

Winston found his classmates bunched around the guinea pigs' table. Their heads at the height of Mrs. Whitestar's shoulders, the children were watching their teacher with worried faces. Looking puzzled, Mrs. Whitestar made no attempt to answer the repeated questions:

"Where are they?"

"What happened?"

"Where did they go?"

"Don't everyone talk at once," she said. "First, go to your seats. There's nothing more to see here."

When she had their attention again, Mrs. Whitestar said, "Now, let's all look carefully around the room. Check by your desks. And in the cupboards."

The children quickly reported that the guinea pigs were nowhere to be found.

"They must have jumped off the table and run out of the room before we got here," Donny suggested.

"Don't be an idiot," Melissa snapped. "If they jumped they'd be killed or break their legs when they hit the floor."

"Yes, I really don't think those guys could go anywhere on their own," Mrs. Whitestar said.

"I think someone's taken them, although I don't know why anyone would steal two guinea pigs. Maybe it's someone's idea of a joke. We'll wait until recess. And then if no one has brought them back, you can go to all the rooms and ask."

"No," a chorus erupted. "We have to find them."

"Let's go now."

"Recess is soon enough." Mrs. Whitestar was firm. "Now take out your books. We have work to do today."

"What's going on?" Caroline whispered as she slid into her seat.

Winston bent down to pick through the plastic bin beneath his desk. "Henry and Mr. Z are gone," he said. "We couldn't find them anywhere in the room."

"That's stupid. Who took them?"

"We don't know." Winston said. "Some *dimwit. A not very bright person. Who sometimes tries to act smart.*" He straightened up, holding a notebook in his hand. "Maybe we'll find out at recess."

Chapter 4

JAMMING AGAINST EACH OTHER AS THEY PUSHED through the door, the children argued about who was going to which classroom. Winston was just behind Mrs. Whitestar, at the end of the line leaving the room. When he got to the door, he turned and was surprised to see Caroline still sitting in her desk. "Come on," he said.

"Where?"

"To look for the guinea pigs."

"Just a sec," Caroline said. She waved her hand to tell Winston to come closer.

"What?" Winston asked.

When he got near to her desk, Caroline said. "I think we should look in this room."

"Here? We already looked here."

"You looked for guinea pigs, and didn't find any. Now I think we should look for clues."

"What do you mean?" Winston asked.

"Someone took Henry and Mr. Z," Caroline said, getting up. "They might have left some clues that will tell us who it was."

"Like what?"

"I don't know. Anything unusual. Do you want to help me look? You take the front of the room. I'll check by the table."

Closing the classroom door, Winston went to peer along the chalkboard ledge. "Just the usual stuff," he said, making a brush into a plough that drove bits of chalk along the ledge. He sneezed. Once. Twice. Three times. "I hate chalk dust," he complained.

Caroline called from under the guinea pigs' table, "Don't go near the board, then. Look somewhere else."

Winston sat down cross-legged on the floor behind Mrs. Whitestar's desk. "We already searched the whole room this morning. We aren't going to find anything." He watched Caroline crawl from underneath the cage and begin a careful course around the outside of the table. "You know," he said, "maybe Mr. Z finally did it."

"What?"

"Made his big escape, and took Henry with him."

"Get serious," Caroline said, her eyes still scanning the floor in front of her. "The only way they could leave this table is if somebody took them. Aren't you going to help?"

Leaning forward, Winston crept under the teacher's desk. "Hey, maybe I found something!" he called.

"What is it?"

"A cigarette lighter."

"Let me see," Caroline said, walking over and kneeling beside him.

Winston turned the tube end over end, then spun the little wheel at the top. "It works," he said as a tiny flame spurted up, then died down. He handed the lighter to Caroline.

Behind them, the classroom door was opened part way then quickly brought back until only a crack showed between the door and its frame.

After jiggling the lighter in her hand, Caroline said, "It's heavy. It must be a good one. Mrs. Whitestar doesn't smoke, does she?"

"No way."

"So unless someone in our room brought it to school, this lighter belongs to whoever took Henry and Mr. Z."

"How did it get under Mrs. Whitestar's desk?"

"It's round. It could roll if it was dropped."

"But it could still be Mrs. Whitestar's," Winston said, "even if she doesn't smoke. Or, maybe the janitor dropped it when he was cleaning."

"Let's keep it," Caroline said, squeezing the lighter.

"But it's not ours."

16

"I know," Caroline said. "I don't mean keep it forever. But let's keep it for awhile and see if we can find out who it belongs to."

The classroom door shut without a sound.

Winston and Caroline were sitting in their desks when Mrs. Whitestar and the rest of their class came back from recess.

Melissa spoke first. "Kristie and I went to tell Mr. Kroop, but he couldn't see us," she announced. "He had someone in the office."

"Melissa," Mrs. Whitestar said. "We really don't need Mr. Kroop's help just yet." To the rest of the class, she said, "Did any of you find out anything?"

As the students shook their heads, Mrs. Whitestar added, "None of the teachers knew anything either. Or if they did, they wouldn't tell me. I still think someone's pulling a joke on us."

"But they might be in danger," Caroline said. "They could die if they're not cared for. They need water and food."

"They should be okay for awhile," Mrs. Whitestar said. "The best thing for us to do is to not panic. If we're patient, I bet we'll have our pets back before too long."

Chapter 5

THE INTRUDER SAUNTERED ALONG THE DESERTED corridor. A yellow plastic bag twirled below one hand. At the door to Mrs. Whitestar's classroom, the intruder stopped. Glancing behind, the intruder bent down and slipped a folded paper part way under the door.

A few steps down the hall, the intruder again checked both directions, then reached over to open one of the lockers. A jumble of books, papers, and clothing started to spill out. The pile was pushed back, the yellow bag squashed into the clutter.

Closing the metal door, the intruder continued down the hallway. It was five minutes before the bell that ended the lunch recess.

Chapter 6

MELISSA WAS THE FIRST PERSON TO GET BACK to the classroom. When she tried the doorknob to see if it was locked, she noticed a bit of paper sticking out from under the door. She pulled out the paper, unfolded it, and read:

Look all you want you'll never find the ginea pigs. They sent you a present. check your lockers

"It's a message!" Melissa gasped. She waved the paper above her head until others looked her way. "It's from the kidnappers. It's about Henry and Mr. Z." Then she held the note close to her chest and refused to show it to anyone else. "It's for Mrs. Whitestar," she insisted. "She has to see it first."

Caroline opened the door to her locker. The heap inside toppled over and slid across her feet. "This is disgusting," she said to Winston. "You've got to tidy it up."

"Yes, I know," Winston said. "I've been thinking about it. Maybe I'll have time after school."

"That's what you always say, but you never do it." Caroline spun around and strode away.

Mrs. Whitestar was taking the piece of paper from Melissa. She had given her keys to Donny, who had just opened the classroom door. Winston closed the metal door and followed his classmates into the room.

When Mrs. Whitestar had read the note, she sighed. "Someone is playing more tricks on us," she said. "Where did you find this?"

Melissa told her. "We should search the lockers right away," she said.

"How come?" Donny asked. "Is that where the guinea pigs are? Is that what it says?"

"You don't have to look in your lockers," Mrs. Whitestar said. "If Henry and Mr. Z were there, they'd have been found by now." She folded the paper and nudged her students aside as she made her way to her desk. "This is getting a little tiresome," she said. "It's taken up too much of our time already."

"No, we should check our lockers!" more children called.

"It won't take long."

"We'll be real fast."

"Please!"

Mrs. Whitestar held up her hands. "Okay, okay. If it's quiet and you all work hard, I'll give you some time just before last recess."

Caroline looked across the aisle. "That," she said, pointing at Winston, "means you."

Before the locker-cleaning began, Mrs. Whitestar read the note out loud.

"That's all it says," she said. "I'm sure I don't know what to expect. I suppose you should look to see if anything is written on another piece of paper. Let me know if you find something."

As some students got up from their desks, Caroline reached down to pick a book from her bin. "Get going, Winston," she said.

"It isn't fair that I have to do it all by myself," he said.

Caroline rolled her eyes. She opened her book to where she was reading. "Tell me when you've got the bottom done, and I'll check my shelf."

"We're finished!" Melissa and Kristie called as Winston went by. "Look at ours first, Mrs. Whitestar. It's perfect." Not far away, Donny had spread his things from one side of the hall to the other. "Winston," he said, "I'm going to go get Mr. Janzen's big tub. Do you want to come?"

"No," Winston said, waving Donny off, "I'd better not. This is going to take awhile." He plucked a book from the pile in his locker. Leafing

21

through its pages, he didn't notice Melissa's sister Melody coming down the hall. A head taller than Winston, Melody had blonde hair that fell below her shoulders.

"Boy, look at you keeners!" Melody said as she got near. With one hand she tucked her hair onto her back. "Anybody need any help?"

"Melody!" Melissa whined, "That's no fair. You can't come along and butt in."

"Don't have a fit, Melissa," Melody said. "I'm just going to get some stuff for Mr. Kroop." She raised her hand and jingled a set of keys in front of Melissa. "He won't mind if I stay for awhile."

"You can help him, then," Melissa said, as Donny returned with the grey tub balanced on one shoulder. "He'll never get done by himself."

"Get lost," Donny growled.

"How are you doing, Winston?" Melody asked. "Need any help?"

"Uh, no," Winston said, looking up from his book. "I'm okay." He picked up another book, which he opened and held on top of the one already in his hand.

"Winston, you're supposed to be cleaning up, not reading," Melissa scolded. "Melody, don't stay, okay? Mrs. Whitestar said I should help."

Melody looked at Winston, then at the inside of his locker. She laughed and turned down the hall. "They're all yours, Melissa," she said.

22

Scrunching loose papers, Donny started to shoot baskets into the tub.

"We have to read those first!" Melissa cried. She reached into the tub. Donny continued to crumple papers and toss them at the barrel. "Donn-nee, this is important," Melissa wailed. "There might be another message. Mrs. Whitestar!"

After reading parts of three more books, Winston noticed the yellow plastic bag. He lifted it up, shook it, and squeezed it, but he couldn't think what it might be. He untied the knot. Inside was a stinking bunch of wood shavings, guinea pig droppings, and soiled newspaper. Winston groaned loudly, made a face, and staggered backwards.

"Too *gross*!" he cried, "*A rotten smell that could make you puke.*"

Expecting someone to laugh at him, he was surprised to find that he was alone in the hall. Beside him, Donny's things had been pushed near the wall, but Donny was gone. Bits of paper on the carpet and an overflowing grey barrel were the only other signs of the cleanup.

Winston found everyone else in the classroom. Keeping the bag at arm's length, he walked to his teacher's desk.

"I think I found it," he said. The other children looked at him. "The stuff from Henry and Mr. Z. It was in my locker. It smells really bad." Winston rolled his eyes as if he was going to faint, and held the bag close to his teacher.

Mrs. Whitestar looked first at Winston, then in the bag. She wrinkled her nose. "Ouuu," she gasped. "Who would do that?"

"What is it?" Donny asked excitedly. "Is it Henry and Mr. Z? Are they dead? Is that why it smells so bad?"

"No, Donny," Mrs. Whitestar said. "It's just some bedding from their table." As the bell sounded for recess, she added, "This is getting pretty sick."

On their way out of the classroom, Caroline asked Winston, "Did you finish?"

"Almost," he answered.

"You did not!" Caroline exclaimed, seeing the few books on the floor and the knee-high mess still inside. "Clean it up now, okay?"

"Where are you going?"

"To ask more people about the lighter. No one's claimed it so far. I'll tell you later what I find out."

Winston watched her start down the stairs, then he picked up the top book from their locker.

Chapter 7

ONE HOUR LATER THE CHILDREN WERE PUTTING away their notebooks for the last time that day. Donny sprinkled shavings over the fresh layer of newspaper on the guinea pigs' table. Near him, Kristie poured pellets into a small bowl.

"What if Henry and Mr. Z aren't back by tomorrow?" Caroline asked.

"I think they will be," Mrs. Whitestar replied. "I have a feeling that the joker's had his fun and tomorrow we'll be right back to normal. Don't worry about it."

The bell rang.

"Winston," Caroline said, "you have to finish the locker before you go. You didn't do anything at recess."

"I ran out of time," he said. When Caroline got up to leave, he offered, "I'll do it now if you stay with me."

"Why should I have to stay?"

"Because then I'll keep at it. When you're not there, I never get as much done."

"I'll stay for ten minutes," she said. "And you really have to work."

"Right," said Winston.

Caroline sat with her back against the wall and pulled a book from her pack. The hallway had emptied quickly.

"What did you find out about the lighter?" Winston asked as he opened the metal door.

"Nothing. It doesn't belong to anyone."

"Have you asked Mr. Janzen?"

"Yes," Caroline said. "But Winston, if I have to stay here, I'm going to read. Don't bother me. We can talk when you're done."

Winston grunted. He began making separate piles for the notebooks and disks and other things he was finding.

After a short while, Mrs. Whitestar walked to the door. "You finally got him to clean that up?" she said to Caroline. "Good for you! But you're going to have to speed it up a bit, Winston. Mr. Kroop is coming by in about fifteen minutes and he won't want to see you here." Mrs. Whitestar went back into the classroom.

"I'll never be done by then," Winston grumbled. "Maybe I should wait until tomorrow."

Caroline sighed and got up. "Sometimes," she said, "you are so useless. Here. I'll go through this stuff. You just put it where I tell you."

Not long after that, Winston was able to place his gym shoes on top of the two binders that sat on the bottom of his locker. He stood back to admire his work. Behind him, Caroline forced a sweater into the top of his bulging backpack.

"All this goes home," she said, tugging the zipper as far across as it would go. "You don't even need it at school. And these," she pointed to a pile of books on the floor, "you take back to the library. Today. And these pencils and things you should keep in your desk. You're always borrowing my stuff."

"See." Winston smiled. "We work so well together."

"We weren't working together," Caroline said. "I did it all for you."

"Actually," he said, "you're lucky. At home I make my mom pay me for doing housework. I did this for free."

"It was all yours."

"But the locker is both of ours, and–"

"Now you can do something for me," Caroline butted in. "My mom wants me to go to her lab and see what she's doing these days. You can walk over to the university with me."

"But I have to carry this backpack home."

"Leave it at my place. I'm going home first. And," Caroline went on before Winston could object, "you can phone from there and tell your mother where we're going."

"What's your mom doing now?"

"She's still a student. But she has this job sorting dinosaur bones. You'd probably like them. Come on, Winston. It's not that far a walk. And my mom will drive us back."

Caroline went into the classroom to put her friend's pencils in his desk. "Bye, Mrs. Whitestar," she said on her way back out.

"You're finished?" Mrs. Whitestar asked. She got up from her desk.

Winston slipped an arm through one of the straps on his backpack. As he heaved it onto his shoulder, Mrs. Whitestar came into the hall.

"Are those all library books!" she exclaimed. She bent down to pick up the pile. "Should we help him with them?" she asked, handing some of the books to Caroline.

When they reached the ground floor, Caroline and Winston followed their teacher into the library. "We'll return these and you can leave before anyone sees you," Mrs. Whitestar said.

"What's that?" A man's voice called out.

Startled, Mrs. Whitestar stopped. Caroline and Winston bumped into her.

"Oh, hi," Mrs. Whitestar said.

Winston peered from behind his teacher to see Mr. Janzen wiping a table top at the far end of the room. He was smiling.

Mrs. Whitestar laid her pile of books on a counter. "I don't suppose you've seen our little pets anywhere?" she asked.

"Not yet." Mr. Janzen turned to face a boy standing a few metres to his side. "Have you?" he asked.

Winston tensed. Slouched against a table, staring back at him, was the one person in the school he hated.

The boy mumbled something and shook his head. Curly red hair cut short, Kelvin wore a faded T-shirt and blue jeans. The shape of a cigarette pack bulged out from his jeans pocket. When he looked at Winston, he seemed to be daring him to say something.

"Kelvin's doing some work for me for a few days," Mr. Janzen explained. "He has to make up for a window he broke yesterday." The janitor waved to Kelvin, who came over to him carrying a spray bottle of cleaner.

"I'll be in my classroom if you find anything," Mrs. Whitestar said as she headed out of the library. "Thanks for looking."

Winston lumbered through the doorway first, right into the path of Mr. Kroop. Weighed down by his swollen pack, Winston almost struck the vice-principal before staggering to a stop.

Mr. Kroop scowled at him.

From behind Winston, Mrs. Whitestar spoke. "Thanks for doing all that tidying up, guys," she said. "Now Mr. Kroop is going to help me find our missing guinea pigs."

"Hmmm." Mr. Kroop reached up to tug his tie sideways. "I was just in your room looking for something I misplaced. You know, I don't like the thought of those animals running loose in the building. I think you should find some other home for them. They really aren't suitable for a school. They're dirty. Smelly. It's not healthy for them to be around children." Mr. Kroop pressed his lips together and pulled once more on his tie.

"Don't you like animals?" Caroline asked.

Mr. Kroop looked down at Caroline as if she'd been invisible until then. "Of course I like animals," he said. "In their place. I grew up on a farm, where animals are kept in the barn."

"But these are—" Caroline stopped when she felt Mrs. Whitestar squeeze her arm. She looked up. Her teacher shook her head, to say a silent "no."

"See you tomorrow," Mrs. Whitestar said, nudging Caroline and Winston through the outside door. "Mr. Kroop and I have things to talk about."

Around the corner of the school, they met Melissa's sister and two other grade eight girls. The three were standing between a large spruce tree and the side of the building.

"Hi guys," Melody said, stepping toward Caroline and Winston. "Too bad about your guinea pigs. You got them back yet?" She reached behind her head to adjust the elastic on her ponytail.

"No," Winston said.

"Melissa said you were cleaning lockers because she found some note."

"There wasn't anything there except some guinea pig droppings," Caroline said.

"Sick-o," Melody said. "Sounds like something Kelvin would do."

Winston nodded his head.

"We found this a while ago," Caroline said, reaching into her pocket. She opened her hand to show the silver tube. "Do you know whose it is?"

Melody dipped her head to peer closely at the lighter. Then she slowly straightened up. "Not mine," she said. "What would I want one of those for?" She smiled at her friends. It looked to Caroline like the kind of smile that shares a secret.

Reaching for the lighter, Melody asked, "Why don't you give it to me? I'll take it to the office for you. We're going there to help Mr. Kroop. He gets us to do stuff because he's busy right now with Mrs. Bobowski away."

Caroline's fingers clamped around the lighter. She jerked her hand away. "No," she said. "I'm going to keep it until I find the owner."

"Suit yourself." Melody shrugged.

31

On her way past where the girls had been standing, Caroline spotted a few cigarette butts ground into the dirt. Some grade eights, she knew, used that place to smoke out of their teacher's view.

Chapter 8

THE HALLS IN THE SCHOOL HAD BEEN STILL FOR almost an hour when the intruder entered the dark room. An old push-button light switch turned on two bulbs that hung on long cords from the ceiling. Following a path between dusty boxes piled on the floor, the intruder walked straight ahead. After about twenty steps, the intruder turned right and entered a second room.

Angled against the walls like raw spaghetti spilled into a pot were about fifty cross-country skis. On the floor were two large open boxes, each holding ski boots tied together in pairs. More boots had been dumped into a tangled pile beside a third box.

The intruder knelt down. A stick of carrot and a few shreds of lettuce stained yellow with mustard dropped into this last box. Henry picked up the carrot with his front paws and started to nibble.

"That's all you're getting for now," the intruder said. "I saved it from my lunch. I'm not coming back for awhile. I can't let anybody see me coming in here." The intruder stood up. "Everything's going just like I planned. You'll be back in your cage in a couple of days." The box was kicked lightly. "Don't stink the place up too much."

Chapter 9

For Winston, the sign on the front door of Caroline's house was more of a gag than a warning. "Beware of dog," it read.

At the top of the steps, Caroline pulled the string holding her house key from around her neck. Winston peered through the window in the door. He could see down a hall to the kitchen at the back of the house. The kitchen table was draped to the floor with a cloth printed with bright green, yellow, and red flowers.

"Beware of dog," Winston muttered.

Caroline turned the key in the lock and opened the door. She stepped inside. Winston followed, closing the door. "Beware of dog," he whispered, looking toward the kitchen.

Both children slipped one arm from their backpack straps. The two bags clumped to the floor.

"Dog?" Winston said, out loud.

From under the tablecloth appeared the brown nose, long, freckled brown and white snout, sad eyes, and droopy ears of an English setter.

"Hi, Grannie," Caroline said. She walked to the kitchen and leaned over to rub behind the dog's ears.

"Oh, don't bother to get up," Winston said cheerfully. "It's just us. It's not a burglar. It's not like you have to defend the house or anything."

"Don't listen to him, Grannie," Caroline said. "You don't have to get up if you don't want to." She nuzzled against the dog's head. A long pink tongue reached out and licked her cheek.

"Someone could be in here and rob the place and be gone, before your dog even woke up," Winston said. "Your dog is, like, in a *coma. Dead to the world. But still breathing.*"

"She barks sometimes," Caroline said. "I think she can tell when it's someone she doesn't know."

Winston crossed the kitchen to lean against a counter. From there, he could see under the table – the tablecloth didn't hang right to the floor on that side. The dog was lying on a cushion in a wicker basket.

"You've always called her Grannie, haven't you?" Winston asked. "Even before she got old."

"It's kind of a nickname," Caroline said, standing up. "She's purebred, so she has this long registered name. Granville Grouser Spruce Farm Kennel ... and some other stuff. Grannie for short."

While she spoke, Caroline picked up a plastic container from the counter. She opened the lid. "Want some?"

"Sure," Winston said, taking three gumdrop cookies. "Thanks."

Grannie swung her head until she was staring at Caroline and Winston. She rested her bottom jaw on the side of the basket.

Caroline picked the chewy gumdrops from her cookies and laid the crumbs on the counter. When she was finished, she scraped the crumbs into the palm of her hand and reached over to feed Grannie. The dog lifted her head, curled her tongue around the crumbs, and pulled the bits of cookie into her mouth.

Turning, Caroline saw a large yellow cat sitting on the outside ledge of the kitchen window. "He's back," she said.

"Who?"

"That cat. We think he's a stray. Mom fed him once, and now he just hangs around. I can let him in if he stays in this room. Do you want to see him?"

"So long as he doesn't get too close. I think I'm allergic to cats."

37

When Caroline opened the back door, the cat jumped down from the window and walked into the kitchen. He sniffed the dog's bowl, then sat on his haunches and looked up at Caroline. *Mmmmrrrup,* he called. Caroline poured some milk into a saucer and placed it on the floor. The cat began licking the milk.

A long, low growl came from Grannie, who was studying the cat with one open eye.

"Isn't Grannie nice?" Caroline said. "That's what she used to do to our old cat. She'd just growl if he got too close."

"Are you going to keep this one?"

"No. My mom just felt sorry for him when he fell out of a tree."

"It fell out of a tree!"

"Mom was doing the dishes and she saw the cat sitting in our tree looking at her. Then when she looked up again the cat was falling through the air. He hit the ground and didn't move. Mom went out to see how he was. When she picked him up, he started to purr a little. So, she brought him inside. And now he thinks he lives here."

The cat strolled over near Grannie, his tail held high. Teeth bared, Grannie snarled.

"It's okay," Caroline said, rubbing the top of the dog's head. "This cat's just visiting. You're still our pet."

Behind her, Winston gasped and quickly

put his hand to his nose as if he was about to sneeze, but he didn't. Caroline picked up the cat, cradled him in her arms, and stroked his fur. She could feel his chest throb as he purred. She carried the cat outside and set him gently on the ground.

Chapter 10

CAROLINE'S HOUSE WAS FIVE BLOCKS FROM THE river running through the centre of the city of Saskatoon. Two more blocks on the street along the river brought them to a railway bridge that crossed the water on seven high towers. The university was a short walk from the other side. Nearby, a waterfall rumbled over a wall, or weir, that was built across the river underwater.

The two friends climbed the steep set of stairs that led to the railway bridge. From the walkway that ran along beside the tracks, they could look down on the water. Ten white pelicans bobbed on the waves churning over at the bottom of the waterfall. Another twenty of the large birds stood together on a sandbar in the middle of the river.

"I thought the pelicans had already gone south for the winter," Winston said.

"They usually have by now," Caroline said. She stopped to lean on the wooden railing. "Look how they're fishing together," she said. "They make a curved line with their bodies to trap fish up against the waterfall."

"Wow," Winston said as one pelican after another dipped its head and long neck into the water.

"My mom says sometimes when they come back up she's seen a fish flapping around inside their bills," Caroline said.

"That'd be neat to see," Winston said, sounding like he wanted to stay and watch the pelicans for awhile longer.

"Except we have to keep going," Caroline said, tugging at his sleeve.

About halfway across the bridge, they passed over the sandbar and the rest of the pelicans. Nearing the other side, Winston muttered under his breath.

"What?" Caroline asked.

"Kelvin," Winston said. "What's he doing down there?"

Below them on the rocky shoreline, the redhead stood staring at the sandbar. Further up the riverbank a bike was propped against a tree. As they watched, Kelvin picked up a rock and heaved it across the water. It plopped into the river short of the pelicans. Kelvin scrambled up the bank, got on his bike, and rode off.

"Looks like he's just watching the pelicans, too," Caroline said.

"Probably trying to kill them, is more like it," Winston said. He knew things about Kelvin that Caroline didn't.

In September, the grade eight boy had moved into a house halfway down the block from Winston. It was about two weeks after school started before he met Kelvin face to face. Crossing the alley that ran behind a confectionery, Winston was almost home. Out of the corner of his eye, he had seen someone move from the side of the building.

"Hey, wait up."

Winston didn't know the skinny kid who shouted the command. He didn't stop.

"Wait up!"

Winston walked a little faster.

"Wilson. I'm talking to you."

Kelvin's shoes scattered gravel as he sprinted to Winston's side.

"That's your name, right?" Kelvin asked, blocking Winston's path.

"Winston," Winston said. He wasn't that much shorter than the other boy, but he was about to learn how much stronger Kelvin was.

"Oh yeah," Kelvin said. "You live near here, don't you?"

"Yes," Winston said. "In the next block."

"Yeah, me too." Kelvin grinned. "Just moved

42

in. Why don't you give your new neighbour a little cash."

"What?"

"Money. Give me some money." Kelvin kept smiling.

"I don't have to give you any money," Winston said, taking a step sideways to try and get past the boy.

"But you're going to." Kelvin's hand shot out to grasp a fold of skin on Winston's shoulder, pinching it through his light jacket. Winston pushed against Kelvin's hand, but the older boy squeezed harder until it hurt Winston like two knives piercing his skin. Winston felt himself being pulled into the alley and held against the wall of the confectionery. Kelvin's other hand slapped his face – not hard but lightly, teasingly.

"You just bought something. I want the change. Empty your pockets."

Grimacing, Winston did as he was told.

"That'll do," Kelvin said. "This is just between you and me, Winston, got it?"

Winston nodded.

"Good." Kelvin released his grip and strolled around the side of the building.

Since then, Kelvin had stopped Winston four or five more times on his way home from the confectionery. He never told his parents. If his mom asked for the change, Winston gave her some of his own money. He hadn't told Caroline about Kelvin, either. He was ashamed to be someone who could be picked on.

At the end of the bridge, Caroline and Winston followed a paved trail that cut across a field to the university. They found Donna, Caroline's mother, sitting cross-legged in a chair just inside the door to a building.

"Hi, guys!" she called, slamming shut the book she was reading. "Right on time. Did Caroline tell you about my new bones, Winston?"

"Sort of."

"We found them on a dig I was on this summer," Donna said. "They might be from a totally new dinosaur. My boss is keeping them hidden until they're sorted and dated, but I can sneak you two in."

"So we'll be the first people to see them?" Winston said. "That's *splendiferous*. *Quite excellent.*"

"Are you sure splendiferous is a real word?" Caroline asked.

"What!" Winston cried, "You don't believe me? Look it up."

Caroline rolled her eyes.

"Come on," Donna said with a smile. "There's a drink machine on the way to my lab. I bet you're thirsty after your hike over the river."

WEDNESDAY

Chapter 11

FROM SOMEWHERE, A VERY LONG WAY OFF, Henry and Mr. Z heard the first faint murmurings of human activity. The morning sun barely lit the four dirty windows high above them.

In cautious spurts and lengthy stops, Henry circled the inside of the box. He ended with his snout in the corner furthest from where Mr. Z slept. With rapid strokes, he pawed at the bottom and side of the box. Fine slivers of cardboard curled off on his claws. He stopped to chew the bits of cardboard, then scraped at the box some more.

Chapter 12

SAFELY THROUGH THE OUTSIDE DOORS, WINSTON crept up the empty stairs on his heels, toes pointed outwards. His classroom door was open, the light shining into the hall. Winston glimpsed inside. What he saw surprised him. Mrs. Whitestar was slumped forward, with her elbows on the desk and her hands cradling her forehead. Winston stopped.

"Mrs. Whitestar?" he asked softly.

His teacher tilted her head, so that her chin now rested in her hands, and looked toward Winston. She seemed very tired, or sad.

"Good morning, Winston." She took a deep breath, then frowned. "You really shouldn't be up here this early, you know."

"Right," Winston said. "I was just getting my journal. I forgot it here yesterday."

"Mmmm," Mrs. Whitestar said. "You can take it back outside if you need to write in it."

She looked down at her desk.

"Is anything the matter?" Winston asked, walking in front of her. Checking the back of the classroom, he saw that the guinea pig cage was still empty. "They're not back yet? Don't worry about them. I bet we find them today. They'll be okay."

"It's not Henry and Mr. Z," Mrs. Whitestar said. "I'm sure we'll get them back. This is worse. Some money has been stolen."

"What money?"

Mrs. Whitestar gazed at Winston. "The money for school T-shirts. Today is the deadline for getting the orders in. When I went to get the cash box from my desk, it was empty. All the money has been taken."

"Wow! Who would do that?"

"I have no idea." Mrs. Whitestar was silent for a moment. "But you'd better leave now." She reached for a tissue. "Mr. Kroop is coming up, and I have to pull myself together before the rest of the kids get here."

The vice-principal, his cheeks a deep red, marched into the room. "What are you doing here?" he barked at Winston.

"I just had to get something," Winston answered.

"Yes, and thank you," Mrs. Whitestar said. "But you should be going now."

"Get downstairs and wait outside for the bell," Mr. Kroop ordered. Yanking his tie back and forth, the vice-principal glared at Winston. "And shut the door behind you."

When the first bell rang, Mr. Kroop was still in the classroom. By the time the second bell sounded, most of Winston's classmates had gathered near the closed door. Winston was sitting in front of his locker, his knees tucked up, reading a book.

Melissa and Kristie came and stood over him.

"So, Winston," Melissa asked, "did you ever get your locker cleaned up?"

"Or did your girlfriend have to help you?" Kristie teased.

"Get lost!" Winston grumbled, whipping his foot toward Melissa's shin.

Melissa jumped aside. "Aw, don't get mad. It's all right if you have a girlfriend." She giggled.

"Hey, two against one. No fair!" Donny cried, coming up behind Melissa. "Leave him alone, or you die!" Donny hunched his back like a gorilla and waved his hands in Melissa's face. "Ahhh!" he jeered.

"You smell like you already died," Melissa spat out. "Why don't you back off!" She stomped down hard on Donny's toes.

"Yow!" Donny yelled. He clutched his aching foot and jumped up and down on one leg. "That really hurt!" Bouncing near Melissa, Donny lunged.

Melissa screamed and threw her arms in front of her face.

"What's going on out here?" Mr. Kroop boomed.

"Donny was trying to hit me," Melissa whimpered.

"Well, he won't be hitting anybody," Mr. Kroop said, tugging at his tie. "Donny, you can come to my office at recess."

"Geez!" Donny groaned.

Melissa lowered her hands to smirk at Kristie.

"Now, inside the room, all of you," Mr. Kroop said. Standing by the entrance to the classroom, he whipped the knot of his tie back and forth.

As Melissa passed by, she said, "Melody won't be here today. She's sick."

"What?" Mr. Kroop said, looking down. "Oh, yes, thank you, Melissa."

Inside the room, Melissa turned to Kristie. "What a liar my sister is. She says she's got the flu. But I know she's just staying home to watch TV and smoke my mom's cigarettes."

Caroline was the last person past the vice-principal.

As the students came into the room, more and more voices called to Mrs. Whitestar.

"They're not back yet!"

"We have to find them!"

"What are we going to do?"

Mrs. Whitestar got up from her chair, walked to the front of her desk, and leaned back on the desktop. Seeing by her face that something was wrong, the children grew quiet.

"I have some bad news," Mrs. Whitestar began.

"They're dead!" Donny called.

"No, it's not about Henry and Mr. Z. Now please listen and don't interrupt until I'm finished. When I went to get the money to pay for your T-shirts, I found that it was gone. The money's been stolen. Someone must have taken it this morning. Someone who knew there would be a lot of money and who knew where to look."

The room was still.

"Will we get our shirts?" Melissa asked.

"I hope so," Mrs. Whitestar replied.

"Who'll pay for them?"

"That I don't know. I suppose it's my fault for leaving the money in my desk. I should've put it in the safe in the office. I just never thought about it being stolen."

"How much was it?" Donny asked.

"Lots. I haven't even added it all up yet."

Chapter 13

AT THE MORNING RECESS, CAROLINE AND WINSTON left the school and drifted across the playground. The grass was still green, but the trees had lost most of their leaves.

"Do you think Mrs. Whitestar will have to pay for all those shirts?" Winston asked. "That's a huge pile of money."

"I know," Caroline answered. "I hope she doesn't. But it's probably that or no one gets a shirt. Or maybe we'll all have to pay again."

When the two friends reached the edge of the schoolyard, they turned, rested their backs against the chain-link fence, and slid down to sit on the ground.

"Who do you suppose did it?" Winston asked.

"I don't know," Caroline said. "Someone who's really cruel."

"Yeah. And probably someone who's stolen stuff before."

"What I can't figure out is why they'd do it. If we knew that, we could probably guess who it was."

"Why they'd do it?" Winston said. "That's easy."

"I have a feeling they're in the school somewhere," Caroline went on. "There must be some other place to look."

"Who's in the school somewhere? What are you talking about?"

"Henry and Mr. Z. They're still missing, remember. We can't just forget about our pets. Whoever was mean enough to take them is probably mean enough to not look after them. We have to get them back."

"What about all the money that was stolen?" Winston asked.

"Let Mr. Kroop worry about it. That's his job. Maybe he already knows who did it." Caroline pointed to the school. "Do you know what that thing is up on the roof?" she asked.

Winston followed her gaze. The school sat like a huge yellow brick block at the other side of the playground. At both ends of the ground floor were double entrance doors. Above the doors, two lines of windows cut across the building. A grey roof rose steeply over the top row of windows. Sticking up from the peak of the roof at the centre of the building was a squat, wooden tower. Painted white, the tower had its own pointed roof and a window at the top of each of its four sides.

"Let's see," Winston said. "The school looks kind of like an old castle. Maybe they used to lock kids up in there. It was a kind of prison on top of the school." When Caroline didn't respond, Winston said, "Right. You want a serious answer." He looked back at the school roof. "How about a *belfry*? *A tower with a bell at the top. Usually found in schools and churches.*"

"I know what a belfry is," Caroline said in an irritated voice. "You don't have to explain it to me."

"Sorry. It's just a habit."

"I wonder how you get to it?" Caroline asked.

"There must be a door somewhere. Why?"

"You might be right about that being a prison. Maybe that's where Henry and Mr. Z are hidden. It's the only place we haven't looked." In a worried tone, she said, "It would be terrible to be locked up in there."

Chapter 14

MRS. WHITESTAR'S STUDENTS WORKED IN A hushed classroom. Her wishes were followed without complaint. The students who usually argued, ignored each other. If they spoke, they talked politely. The questions that needed to be asked were held until just before lunchtime.

"Did you find out who did it, Mrs. Whitestar?"

"No."

"What's Mr. Kroop going to do?"

"I don't know."

"Are we going to get our shirts?"

"I hope so."

"Who'll pay for them?"

"I don't know yet. Hopefully we'll get the money back from whoever took it."

When the bell rang, the children left quickly. Caroline was going to her house to eat with her mom. That morning, Winston's mother had given him some money to buy milk to bring home for lunch. From the instant he had taken the five-dollar bill, Winston had been dreading the noon recess. He was sure he would be robbed.

As he left the confectionery, Winston steeled himself to get past the alley. Kelvin wasn't there. Sure that he was safe, Winston relaxed on the block before his house.

"Wilson!"

Winston was jolted as if he'd been hit. Kelvin was ambling down the front steps of the house he lived in. He paused to take a cigarette from his jeans pocket, stick the tip of the filter between his lips. He slapped his pockets, then stepped around a bicycle and stood on the sidewalk in Winston's path.

I'm not going to stop, Winston told himself. If he tries to grab me, I'll run. I can make it home from here.

"Wilson," Kelvin said. "How's it going?"

Winston didn't answer. His shoulder started to ache.

"Hey, what's the trouble?" Kelvin said, pretending to sound concerned. "I've just got to ask you something." When he spoke, Kelvin looked like a tough guy in a movie, his cigarette bobbing from his lips. "You got a match, Wilson?"

"Winston. What? No."

"Didn't think you would." Kelvin took a short step backwards off the sidewalk and brought his open hands up in front of his chest. "No problem. You go ahead. I'm not looking for trouble." He smiled. "You can even keep your money today."

As Winston went by, Kelvin's fist flashed toward his shoulder. Winston grimaced. Kelvin's knuckles struck a soft, playful tap.

"Take it easy," Kelvin said.

Winston was past. His heart still beating wildly, he thought about how Kelvin treated him. He gets a big kick out of *tormenting people. Causing pain. Torturing.*

Chapter 15

HENRY'S CLAWS PIERCED THE TORN CARDBOARD and snagged briefly in the hard wooden surface below. A few more strokes and a tiny hole appeared in the bottom of the box. Henry sat back to nibble cardboard shavings from his claws.

At the other end of the box, Mr. Z stirred from his sleep. Slowly he waddled over to chew on the bit of wrinkled carrot. Leaving his corner, Henry joined Mr. Z. After they each had eaten a bit of the carrot, the two guinea pigs lay down side by side and went to sleep.

Chapter 16

EVERYONE IN MRS. WHITESTAR'S CLASS WAS working on a science report. Paired with her friend Heather, Caroline was one of the first to finish her written part. She closed her notebook and went to where her teacher was helping Donny. Mrs. Whitestar looked up.

"I need some drawing paper," she said. "For my picture. Can I go get some?"

"Sure," Mrs. Whitestar replied, "that's a good idea. Other kids will need some, too. You'll have to go to the art room where the good paper is kept." Mrs. Whitestar slipped the coiled plastic bracelet with her key ring off her wrist. "The long, silver one is for inside doors," she said, holding the key out to Caroline. "Come right back."

"Thanks," Caroline said. Seeing that Mrs. Whitestar was again bent over Donny's desk, she waved at Winston to follow her.

In the hallway, Caroline explained. "I've found the way to that tower. Mr. Janzen says there's a door in his supply room." She looked down the corridor. "The one right there, across from the staff room."

"Really?" Winston asked. "I've cleaned brushes in there and I've never seen a door."

"Me neither. He says there's usually a pile of boxes in front of it, because its not used very much. Just to store stuff."

"How did you get him to tell you?"

"I just asked. I never said why I wanted to know. I guess there's a big room back there with a ladder up to the tower. And you were right, there did used to be a bell, but not any more."

"But the supply room is always locked. You need a key to get in."

"Like this one?" Caroline asked, smiling and holding up her hand. Mrs. Whitestar's bracelet circled her wrist.

"How'd you get that?"

"I have to go to the art room to get some paper. If we hurry we'll have time to look in the supply room before we go back. Come on."

Caroline headed down the hall. Winston thought about the report waiting on his desk. In a moment, he hurried after Caroline.

They rushed down two flights of stairs to the basement. After opening the art room, Caroline pushed the lock on the handle while Winston found some paper. She closed the door behind him and they ran back to the stairs, climbing in quick, noisy steps.

At the top floor, they stopped, panting, to peer down the corridor.

"What happens if we get caught?" Winston asked.

"We'll be careful."

"Yes, but...."

"We have to hurry, before Mrs. Whitestar wonders where we are."

"Okay, but you go first," Winston said, propping one arm against the wall. "I'm still out of breath."

Caroline scowled. She started walking toward their classroom. At the open door to the staff room, a sideways glance told her the room was empty. She stepped across the hall and stuck the key in the door to the supply room. When it opened, Winston was right behind her. He closed the door.

"Over here," Caroline said. She tugged a stack of boxes a little way out from the wall. Winston could see a door frame. "Help me," Caroline said.

Winston laid the papers on a counter beside the machine used to clean chalk brushes. He gripped the corners of the top two boxes. Together they moved the pile a few centimetres from the wall. One side of the door and the doorknob were now visible.

"I think I can reach it," Caroline said, stretching an arm behind the pile of boxes. "It's not locked." She straightened up. "We can come back later."

"Let's just get out of here," Winston said, looking toward the door. "We'll be nailed if anyone catches us."

After sliding the pile back into place, and peeking out the door, Caroline and Winston left the supply room. As they neared their classroom, Caroline looked down at Winston's hands.

"Where's the paper?" she asked.

"Oops," Winston said, "I left it back there. Let's just forget it."

"We can't. That's why I got the keys. Mrs. Whitestar will ask why I don't have it."

"You go back and get it then," Winston said, edging toward the classroom door. "I'll wait here."

"You go, Winston," Caroline replied firmly. "You were supposed to bring it." She pressed Mrs. Whitestar's bracelet into Winston's palm.

Winston slouched back down the hall. He opened the supply room door and stepped inside, leaving the door slightly ajar.

Just as he disappeared from view, Mr. Kroop and the janitor came down the hall from the far set of stairs. Caroline moved to her locker, opened the door, and pretended to be looking for something.

It will take Winston just a couple of seconds to get the paper, she thought. He's going to walk out right in front of Mr. Kroop. She sneaked a look over her shoulder. The vice-principal was talking to Mr. Janzen.

As they got closer to her, Caroline heard Mr. Kroop say, "…tell me if you find it. I don't use it that much, but I've had it a long time. It's going to bother me until I get it back." Then he jerked his necktie sharply back and forth.

If Winston opens the door now, Caroline thought, Mr. Kroop will bump right into it. But without a glance at either her or the door, Mr. Kroop led the janitor into the staff room. The door behind them opened.

When he came into the hall, Winston was watching Caroline. He kept looking in her direction as he closed the door. By the time he started down the hall, the two men were out of sight in the staff room.

A few steps from her, Winston suddenly put his hand to his nose and sneezed – once, twice, three times. "Chalk dust," he said. "It always makes me sneeze."

Chapter 17

A T THE END OF SCHOOL THAT DAY, MRS. Whitestar still couldn't answer questions about the missing money.

"I really don't know what will happen," she said in a way that made it clear she was tired of being asked. "I'm going to see Mr. Kroop after school. I know he's very concerned about it too. Maybe he'll have found out something."

"Well," Melissa said loudly, "I know my mom's going to be really mad. She'll want to know who's going to pay for my shirt. She'll make Mr. Kroop do something."

Winston knew Melissa was probably right. He'd seen her mother storm into the school and yell at teachers for doing something Melissa or Melody didn't like.

"I don't think this means you won't get your shirts," Mrs. Whitestar said, sounding like she wasn't at all sure. "Today was kind of a deadline for getting the money in. But there's still time for ordering. Maybe the money will show up, or...." She faltered.

"Maybe we could have a pizza day to raise money," someone suggested.

"Or a garage sale," Winston said. "We could each sell stuff we don't want any more."

"We could sell Melissa then," Donny said, "if anyone would buy her."

"We could sell you to the SPCA, dog breath," Melissa sneered.

"Please stop." Mrs. Whitestar spoke in a tired voice. "We've made it through the day without fighting. Don't start now. You're dismissed. Have a nice night. Let's hope tomorrow doesn't bring any more bad news."

As her classmates began leaving the room, Caroline approached her teacher's desk. Mrs. Whitestar was closing her books and stacking papers in neat piles.

"Winston and I could clean the room today," Caroline said.

"Well," Mrs. Whitestar said, "you really shouldn't be here after school. Especially with all this stuff being stolen."

"It won't take us long. We'll just tidy up a bit and wipe the boards."

"I don't know, Caroline. I can't be here. I have to get right down to the office."

"We'll keep the door closed and stay in the

room. Wouldn't you like it to look good when we come back tomorrow morning?"

"Yes," Mrs. Whitestar agreed, looking around, "that would be nice. Our room has been getting kind of messy this last while."

Mrs. Whitestar got up from her desk and straightened her skirt and blouse. "You mustn't go out in the hall, okay?" She walked to the door, turned and held the doorknob. "And, keep this shut. And don't take too long. Mr. Kroop might come back up with me." Before the door closed all the way, she added, "Thanks, guys."

"I think Mr. Janzen leaves the supply room open after school," Caroline said when she and Winston were alone. "When we get this done, we can watch for a chance to sneak down there."

Winston stayed put. "This," he said, "is not a good idea. What it is, is *ludicrous. Being so stupid it almost makes you laugh.* I don't mind looking for Henry and Mr. Z with you, but I'm not going to clean up after other people." Frowning, Winston licked the tips of his fingers and rubbed at the tuft of hair on the side of his head.

"Come on. Just help a little," Caroline said, as she crawled down an aisle. The books and pieces of paper she picked up were dropped into the plastic bins sitting under the desks.

"I hate cleaning up."

Caroline finished one aisle and turned to start down another. "Do the boards, then. Just

65

do something, and then we can go to the supply room."

With a sigh, Winston hauled himself up from his desk and plodded to the front of the room. Picking up a brush, he made long, curving strokes on the chalk board. Halfway across, he stopped and sneezed, three times. "I'm definitely allergic," he said, and dropped the brush on the ledge.

Winston walked to the door. He listened for any noises coming from the hallway. Hearing none, he peeked out. The corridor was empty.

"It's all clear," he said, pulling the door closed again. "And the room's open. Let's go."

"Just a sec."

Caroline straightened books on a shelf beneath the windows before she joined Winston. He took one step into the hall then quickly retreated back.

"He's there," he said.

"Who? Mr. Kroop?"

"No. Kelvin. He must still be helping Mr. Janzen." Winston pulled the door closed. "I think he's the one who took Henry and Mr. Z, you know."

"You do? How come?"

"Two good reasons. One. He's always wrecking things that aren't his – like that window he broke. And two. He smokes. That's probably his lighter that we found."

"Maybe. I haven't asked him about it yet. If Mr. Janzen's out there, we probably should go. I don't want to get Mrs. Whitestar in trouble."

The hall was empty again except for the janitor's cart. Leaving the classroom behind Caroline, Winston saw Kelvin carrying a metal wastebasket to the cart. As he lifted the basket to dump the contents into a grey bin, a ring of janitor's keys flashed in Kelvin's hand. Winston hurried down the steps.

Chapter 18

THE YELLOW CAT CALLED FROM HIS PERCH IN A tree when Caroline and Winston were almost at her front door. *Mmmmrrrup.*

"Let's see if he'll come for me," Caroline said. She stretched her hand up toward the branch. "Kittykittykitty," she called.

The cat crawled down the tree trunk to a lower limb. Caroline could almost touch him. "Come kitty," she said.

Mmmmrrrup, the cat called. He jumped off the branch – and away from Caroline's hands. The cat fell heavily to the ground near Winston's feet.

Caroline reached down, gently picked up the cat, and cradled him in her arms. The cat stayed limp.

"Open the door," Caroline said, pulling the key string from around her neck. "He might be injured."

In the kitchen, Caroline kept petting the cat while Winston looked for a saucer for milk. When Winston pulled on the fridge door, the cat opened his eyes and purred weakly.

Caroline laid the cat on the floor beside the saucer. He raised himself on his haunches and began to lick the milk.

"Why did he do that?" Winston asked.

"He's just a weird cat," Caroline said. She scratched Grannie behind the ears. Without opening her eyes, the dog lifted her head so Caroline could reach under her chin. "Want some more of those cookies?" she asked, standing up.

"Sure," Winston said. He sat down at the kitchen table.

"We can't wait until tomorrow to find Henry and Mr. Z," Caroline said. "If they haven't had any food or water, that might be too late. We have to find them today."

"But the school will be locked by now," Winston said.

"Now," Caroline said, "but not tonight. There are meetings there almost every night. They must keep the door open for people to get in."

"I don't think that's such a good idea. We're not supposed to be there at night."

"No one will see us. The meetings are in the library. We'll be upstairs."

"Well, actually," Winston said, glancing at his pack near the front door, "I was going to do some homework tonight. Right after supper."

"Do it now," Caroline said.

"Huh?"

"You can work at this table," Caroline said. "That's what I do." She picked up the plastic cookie container. "There. You can do it before you go home."

"But...."

"In fact, you can stay here for supper. It's lasagna. I know because its frozen and I have to put it in the microwave at five. I'll call my mom and let her know."

"But...."

"Just phone your mother. Tell her you're invited for supper. And that my mom will drive you home later."

Winston knew that Caroline would get her way. "Okay," he said, "you win. But don't get your mom to drive me home. I'll walk. And you can say you'll come with me to keep me company. That will be our excuse to be out together tonight."

"Excellent!" Caroline cried.

Winston shook his head slowly and pushed himself off the chair. "I hope so," he said. "Because if we get caught we'll be as dead as that cat."

Caroline looked down at the cat sprawled on the floor beside Grannie's basket. "Maybe he needs a comfy place to lie," she said. She scooped him into her hands. "There's room in Grannie's basket." Caroline laid the cat on a part of the cushion that wasn't covered by the sleeping dog.

Grannie opened one eye and growled.

"It's just until he's feeling better," Caroline said, patting the dog's side.

The cat raised his back legs, stuck out the claws in his front paws, and stretched his body flat. He stepped over to the dog and poked his paws into Grannie's haunches. Then he lay down, using the dog's body as if it was his own big bean bag.

Grannie shifted her body further into the curve of her bed. With a deep sigh, her head slipped over the side of the basket to rest on the floor.

Winston trudged to the front door to get his backpack. Caroline strolled toward the living room at the front of the house.

"I'm going to watch some TV," she said. "My mom tapes the soaps for us. I'll keep the sound down until you're finished."

Winston let the pack slip from his hands. "Which soaps do you watch?" he asked, stepping into the living room.

Chapter 19

CAROLINE AND WINSTON LEANED AGAINST THE dark trunk of a tall tree that grew on one edge of the playground. On the far side of the yard, a street lamp, partly hidden in the branches of other trees, cast a feeble light. They'd been standing there for ten minutes, long enough to get chilled through their sweaters.

Every minute or so, a bright beam had cut across the playground as a car turned into the school parking lot. Shortly after, a shadow had hurried from the car toward the school. When each figure neared the building, it had been lit briefly by the light above the door nearest the parking lot.

"No one's come for awhile," Caroline said. "Do you think we should go in now?"

"Probably." Winston shivered. "I think they lock the door when everyone's there."

They ran to the entrance. Once inside, Winston held the door so that it clicked softly behind him. Through a window in a door, they glimpsed the meeting taking place in the library. Caroline and Winston ducked below the window and scurried softly up a flight of stairs. The top floor hallway looked murky, like a place underwater. As they passed each doorway, faint light from the outside windows lit their faces.

Winston found the supply room door. When they were both inside, Caroline touched the light switch. Squinting in the sudden brilliance, Winston began moving the boxes hiding the door to the storeroom. When the pile had been cleared away, Caroline opened the door. She and Winston peered inside. By the light from the supply room, they could make out boxes stacked on the floor near the door. Everything else in the room was in shadow.

"It's dark in there," Winston said.

Reaching around the corner, Caroline felt rough, cracked plaster, then a smooth metal plate. A tube that was about as thick as a piece of chalk stuck a few centimetres out from the plate. She pushed on the tube and the lights burst on.

"I don't see our guinea pigs," Winston said.

"We'll have to look," Caroline answered. She walked across the room. "Where would someone put those guys?" she asked out loud. "Do you

73

think they might be inside a box that's closed up?" She pried open the top flaps of a box. "Old books," she said. She kicked a few nearby piles. "These must be too. They're all pretty heavy."

"Maybe this isn't the right place," Winston said. "Wasn't there supposed to be a ladder going up to the tower on the roof?"

"You're right," Caroline said. "Maybe there's another room. I think there's a door back here." She hurried to the furthest wall. "There is. Come on, Winston."

Caroline pushed on the door until, about half open, it struck against something behind it. "They're here!" Caroline called, recognizing the sour smell of guinea pig droppings. In the dim light she knelt and reached into an open box. Henry scrambled to sniff her fingertips. She scooped him into her palm and stood up.

"Let me see." Winston pulled on Caroline's sweater. When she stepped back into the doorway holding Henry close to her chest, Winston ruffled the little creature's fur. Then he pressed by to lift Mr. Z behind the front legs and under the rump. Pulling Mr. Z up under his chin, Winston gently stroked the guinea pig from head to tail. "It's okay," he said softly. "It's okay. You're going to be fine now."

"Wow! Are they happy to see us," Caroline said. "His little heart's going about a thousand times a minute."

"Same with Mr. Z." Winston looked down at the box where the two animals had been kept. "There's no food for them. They must be starving. And their bedding's really dirty."

Still holding Henry against her chest, Caroline walked across the store room. "I saw some pet things over in this corner," she said. "Maybe there's something they can eat." Keeping one hand on the guinea pig, she peered into a large box. "There's an aquarium," she said, "and some coloured pebbles. A box of fish food. They can't eat that."

She reached into the box to tug at a wire cage. "Here's a gerbil cage and one of those exercise wheels. There's something underneath it." Caroline pulled on the cage. "It's stuck," she said. Wrapping her fingers through the wire mesh, she yanked her arm upward. The cage sprang from the box, catching on the top flap. The tin bottom separated from the cage and crashed onto the floor.

"Sshh!" Winston hissed. "They'll hear us."

"I didn't do it on purpose," Caroline answered crossly. She balanced the cage on top of the aquarium, then pulled a small jar from the bottom of the box.

Holding it close to her face, she said, "Gerbil food. This'll do for two hungry guinea pigs." She joined Winston.

"The ladder's in there all right," he told her.

"Nailed to the wall. It goes straight up as far as you can see."

"I'm glad they weren't hidden up there," Caroline said. "Let's see if they'll eat this stuff." She put Henry back in the empty box and shook some of the dry pellets out of the jar. Henry took one in his paws.

"Eat up, Mr. Z," Winston said as he laid the other guinea pig beside Henry. "They'll need water, too."

"There's a sink in the other room where Mr. Janzen washes his mops," Caroline said, getting up.

Winston followed Caroline to the supply room. "There's this," he said, handing her a metal jar lid from the counter. "But maybe they need a water bottle."

"They don't have any choice," Caroline said, twisting open a tap to fill the lid with water.

"And here's a roll of paper towels," Winston said.

Soon after, Henry was stepping carefully across the bumpy paper that now covered his box. At one end, dry food was sprinkled beside the jar lid. Mr. Z was lying, apparently asleep, at the other.

Winston stroked Mr. Z's fur. "I wish we didn't have to leave you here," he said. "But we can't take you with us."

"It's just until tomorrow," Caroline said.

"Then we'll let Mrs. Whitestar know where they are."

On the way out, Caroline snapped the store-room light switch off and closed the door. Together, they re-piled the boxes.

Winston walked past the brush cleaner to the door leading into the hallway. He flicked off the light switch, put his hand on the doorknob – then froze. "Voices!" he whispered. "There's someone out there. And," he gasped once, twice, "I'm going to sneeze!"

Chapter 20

C AROLINE'S PALM HIT WINSTON'S FACE SO HARD, little stars flashed in front of his eyes. Before he had time to complain, her fingers squeezed off his breath. Somehow his hand found the light switch. When the bulb flashed on and she could see he wasn't going to sneeze, she let go.

"Ow!" He mouthed the word, and rubbed his nose.

"Sorry," Caroline whispered.

In a moment, Caroline had her hand on the doorknob. She nodded at Winston to turn off the light again. Then she shouldered the door open until there was a sliver of light shining in between the side of the door and the doorframe.

After a few seconds she pulled the door closed. "The lights are on," she whispered to Winston. "Mr. Kroop was going down the hall with some other guy. He said something about it being ready in five minutes."

"Mr. Kroop is here?" Winston asked. "Just our luck. They must be making coffee in the staff room."

Caroline checked the corridor again. It was empty. She and Winston ran on tiptoes to the top of the stairs farthest from their classroom. Still on tiptoes, they started down the steps, lit only by the lights from the upstairs hallway.

Safely past the dark first-floor landing, they made a dash for the outside exit. Without slowing down, Winston threw his hip against the door. The metal bar crashed against solid steel. The door stayed firmly shut.

"Oooohh," Winston moaned, sliding to the floor.

Caroline reached over him. "It's chained shut," she said. "Are you okay?"

"I don't think so. My leg...."

"You have to get up." She gripped Winston's arm. "They must have heard that all over the school. Come on."

"I don't think I can."

"You have to. Do you want Mr. Kroop to catch us?"

Rubbing his aching leg with the palm of his hand, Winston staggered upright. "Now what do we do?" he asked.

"If we go down through the basement we can get out the other side," Caroline said.

"But the people from the meeting will be coming out there."

"Maybe it won't be over yet." Caroline led her hobbling friend down another darkened stairway. At the bottom, they stepped through a door and found themselves bathed in the dim red light of an EXIT sign.

"Geez," Winston murmured, "spooky, or what?"

The hallway was a narrow tunnel with concrete walls that ran from one side of the school to the other. Heating pipes hung from the ceiling. Doors led to classrooms, washrooms, and the janitor's office. The only light came from the EXIT signs at both ends of the corridor.

Caroline caught Winston's sleeve. They walked without speaking until their faces were lit by the red light at the far door.

"I'll look," Caroline offered. She opened the door a crack to see the set of stairs that led to the school exit. They were a few steps from a safe escape.

"After you," she said. "I'll hold the door."

Shielding his eyes from the light, Winston stepped through the doorway.

"What are you doing down there?" a man bellowed from the top of the stairs.

Winston lurched to a stop. His heart caught. He knew who it was without looking up. He backed up into the hallway and twisted around.

Red light played on Caroline's fleeing back. He sped off after her.

He was halfway down the tunnel before Mr. Kroop roared again. "Hey! Stop right now! Come back here!"

Winston raced on.

Suddenly he sensed a movement at his side. "In here!" Caroline called. Her outstretched fingers brushed against his shoulder.

When Winston put out his hand, it caught on an open door. He skidded and bumped to a stop against the wall, then hauled himself backwards and stepped through the doorway. In the moment it took for the door to close behind him, lights flashed on along the hall and into the room. Not daring to speak, Winston stared into Caroline's eyes. Then there was total darkness.

They didn't move. Soon Mr. Kroop's shoes slapped closer in the corridor. The steps slowed down outside their door. "Get back here!" he yelled. "You can't get away."

And then, for many heartbeats, they heard nothing.

"Is he still out there?" Caroline whispered in a quivery voice.

"I don't know. I didn't hear him go. We'd better wait here for awhile."

After what might have been a minute, but seemed like fifty, Caroline spoke – so softly Winston could barely hear her.

"Winston," she said.

"Yes," he answered from the blackness.

"I'm scared." Caroline shakily drew in her breath. "Really scared."

"Me, too. He almost caught me."

"It's not Mr. Kroop I'm afraid of – it's the dark."

"The dark?"

"Yes. I can't stand it when I can't see anything. I've always been like that. My mind just goes crazy-scared." Caroline took a loud, ragged breath. "I think I'm going to cry."

Caroline felt Winston touch her arm. Then his hand closed around hers.

"Hey, it's going to be okay," he said.

"But I can't see anything," Caroline whimpered.

Winston pulled Caroline's free hand away from her side. "Here, look at this," he said. Caroline heard a tiny scratchy ticking sound. Then a circle of small green numbers appeared a few centimetres in front of her face.

"Can you see that?" Winston asked. "It's my dad's old wind-up watch. He found it in a box of junk and gave it to me. You hold it. Just keep looking at the numbers."

Caroline was quiet.

"Is it working?" Winston asked.

"Yes. When I get it really close to my eyes, the numbers fill up the whole space."

"*Nyctophobia.*"

"What?"

"*Nyctophobia. Fear of the dark.* That's what you have."

"Oh."

"Where are we anyway?"

"The girls' washroom."

"Really?" Winston snorted, then quickly covered his mouth. "The girls' washroom? I got saved by running into the girls' washroom?"

"You almost missed it too. I didn't think you could run that fast." Caroline giggled. "How's your sore leg?"

"I didn't feel a thing as soon as I took off," Winston said. "I still don't feel it."

"Can we go yet?" Caroline asked, serious again. "Do you think Mr. Kroop is out there?"

"No. He's probably looking for us somewhere else. Now's our chance."

Winston pulled Caroline toward the closed door. "Here we go," he said. With one quick look up and down the hall, he led Caroline out of the washroom. "If someone sees us, we run for it."

They race-walked to the exit door at the end of the hall. Winston hesitated only an instant before starting up the stairs, their scraping footsteps echoing loudly. At the top, neither one looked toward the meeting room. No one called to them. The outside door opened easily.

"Keep going," Winston said.

They hustled through the circle of light and

didn't stop until they were nearly at the far side of the yard. Their hands separated as they turned back to face the school.

Winston shook his arms at his sides. "My fingers are sore," he said.

"Mine, too. You were squeezing really hard."

"Me? You're the one who was squeezing. I thought you were going to break my knuckles like you almost broke my nose."

Caroline giggled. "Let's not do that again for awhile, okay?" she said.

"Deal," Winston said. "Do you think he recognized us?"

"No. He couldn't have. It was dark down there."

"Not when I walked through the door and he yelled at me. He saw me then."

"That was just for a second. If he'd recognized you, he would've called your name."

"You think so?" Winston wasn't convinced.

"Sure," Caroline said, heading toward a dark lump near the playground fence. "There's nothing to worry about." She picked up the lump and handed it to Winston. "And you still have lots of time to do your homework."

"Aw," Winston groaned, and slung his backpack over one shoulder.

THURSDAY

Chapter 21

THE DOOR TO THE JANITOR'S SUPPLY ROOM SLAPPED shut. The intruder pushed the lock button in the centre of the door knob. A plastic bag dropped onto the counter near the storeroom door. The pile of boxes was shifted to one side.

Entering the storeroom, the intruder punched on the light switch and walked to the entrance to the little room. After taking a leaf of lettuce and two carrots from the plastic bag, the intruder elbowed open the door.

"Here's something to keep you alive, you…."

The intruder stopped at the sight of the metal lid of water, the little mound of pellets, the paper towels. "Oh, _____," the intruder swore.

"Someone else wants to feed you, let them. You won't see me back here again." The lettuce and carrots and plastic bag fell to the floor outside the guinea pigs' box. "I don't need you any more, anyway."

The boxes in front of the storeroom door were replaced. The hallway door was opened, then closed.

Once more in the dark, Henry shuffled to a corner of the box. His sharp claws lifted an edge of the paper towel. Part of the paper tore away to show the hole in the cardboard below. From somewhere near came the scent of fresh food. He crept further into the corner and clawed at the side of the box. At the other end of the carton, Mr. Z slept.

Chapter 22

THE PHONE RANG WHILE WINSTON WAS EATING breakfast. It was Caroline. "We have to talk," she said.

"About what?"

"I've been thinking about how we're going to tell Mrs. Whitestar about Henry and Mr. Z. If we tell her how we found them, Mr. Kroop will find out we were in the school last night."

"So what do you suggest?" Winston asked.

"I don't know, but let's not say anything until we get a chance to talk, okay?"

"Sure. Can you come to school early?"

"No. We just got up. Maybe at recess."

Winston agreed, not knowing that when he talked to Caroline again the guinea pigs would be far from his mind.

Chapter 23

MR. KROOP WAS STANDING BESIDE MRS. Whitestar outside the classroom door as the nine o'clock bell rang. "It's been gone for a couple of days," he said. "And I really want to get it back. Maybe you could look out for it, too."

"Oh, sure," Mrs. Whitestar said. "What does it look like?"

"Well," Mr. Kroop said, "it's about the usual size." He held his thumb and forefinger a few centimetres apart. "And it's shiny silver."

The vice-principal tugged on his tie and stuck his head through the open doorway. "You have to admit," he said, "your room's lost that unpleasant smell now that those guinea pigs aren't in there. It was probably time to get rid of them anyway."

"But the kids really miss them," Mrs. Whitestar said, as the first of her students entered the room.

Mr. Kroop's face began to darken to a deep red. "You know," he said, "there was more trouble again last night. Things are really falling apart around here. Maybe it's just as well that Mrs. Bobowski is away. She's getting kind of old for this stuff." He jerked his tie. "Good thing I'll have everything under control by the time she gets back."

"What else has happened?" Mrs. Whitestar asked.

"Some vandals snuck into the school during the parents' meeting."

Listening from his locker, Winston couldn't move. His ears locked onto the vice-principal's words.

"Did they do any damage?" Mrs. Whitestar asked.

"No. Luckily I found them before they had a chance."

"Did you catch them? Who was it?"

"They got away, but I've an idea who it was."

"Oh?" Mrs. Whitestar sounded like she was losing interest. "Come on, kids," she called to the students who were still in the hall. "You should be in the room by now."

Winston forced himself to close his locker. He saw Mrs. Whitestar go into the room. He held back until Donny was on his way to the door. As they got close to the vice-principal, Winston looked steadily at Donny's back.

"Winston!" Mr. Kroop stopped him. Donny went further into the room, then turned and walked out of sight. Winston felt all alone, like there was just him and this man in the whole school. He faced Mr. Kroop, looking straight at the vice-principal's chest. The hand whipping the tie from side to side was a blur. He watched the knot of the tie digging further into the purple flesh of Mr. Kroop's neck.

"You'll come with me," Mr. Kroop said.

"What? I didn't do anything," Winston protested.

"Come with me," Mr. Kroop repeated. He strode toward the stairs.

When Mr. Kroop reached the principal's office, he stopped. With his hand on the door-knob, he pointed to a chair near Mrs. Bobowski's desk. Mr. Kroop closed the door and sat behind the desk in a large cloth-covered chair.

Winston's heart was racing. Mr. Kroop knew it was him who had been in the school. What would happen to him? he wondered. Would his parents find out?

"You and I need to have a serious talk, young man," Mr. Kroop began. "You've been seen in this school at times when you should not have been here."

Winston was silent. He watched his thumb picking at a loose piece of skin near a fingernail. But he couldn't feel anything, like the hands weren't really his.

"Yesterday you were in the upstairs hall before the nine o'clock bell, right?" Mr. Kroop asked.

"Um, yes," Winston answered. What does that have to do with anything? he wondered.

"You know there's a rule about not coming in before the bell goes?"

"Yes," Winston said. He felt his chest relax. That was all Mr. Kroop was upset about.

"So, why were you there?"

"I had to get something."

"You had to get something," Mr. Kroop repeated. "What did you have to get?"

"A book," Winston said. "I had to get a book to take back to the library, so I could get another book for reading time."

Mr. Kroop wrote something on a yellow pad of paper in front of him.

This isn't so bad, Winston thought.

"You often come into school before the bell, don't you?"

"I guess so."

"And sometimes you go into your classroom before your teacher gets there. Is that right?"

"Not much. Usually Mrs. Whitestar is there first."

"Usually ... but sometimes...." Mr. Kroop paused. His fingers clutched the knot of his tie and jerked it away from his skin.

"Now, Winston," he went on, sounding kinder.

"I'm glad you're being so honest and telling me the truth about this. But I wonder if there isn't something else you'd like to tell me? Hmmm?"

Should I admit it was me in the school last night? Winston asked himself. Maybe it would be all right. Mr. Kroop didn't seem to be too mad any more about him coming into school early.

Before Winston could answer, Mr. Kroop continued. "You know, Winston, that some money is missing from Mrs. Whitestar's desk?"

"Yes," Winston said. This is okay, he thought. Now he wants me to help him find the money.

"And you know that the money was stolen early yesterday morning."

"Yes."

"Well, what else do you know about that?"

"Not much. Mrs. Whitestar just told us it had been taken."

"It was a lot of money."

"About five hundred dollars, I guess."

Mr. Kroop raised his eyebrows. With his pencil poised, he asked, "How do you know that? Mrs. Whitestar never told anyone how much it was."

"Just..." Winston began, his mouth suddenly dry, "just because it was T-shirt money. And that's how much it would be if most kids bought one."

Leaning forward, Mr. Kroop softened his tone even more. He could have been talking to a baby. "Whoever took that money was in the school early yesterday morning, Winston. You've already told me you were here then. Isn't there something else you'd like to say?"

The vice-principal paused and pushed back in the chair. "You like Mrs. Whitestar, don't you?" he asked. "She's always been kind to you, hasn't she? Well, this is bad for her, you know, very bad. That's a lot of money for her to make up. You wouldn't want her to have to pay back that five hundred dollars by herself, would you? What could you do to help her, hmmm?"

"I don't know," Winston croaked. What Mr. Kroop was now saying was getting scary.

The vice-principal tugged at his tie. "If the money comes back," he said, "there'll be no questions asked. That's my policy." Mr. Kroop smiled coldly.

"I ... I didn't take the money," Winston stammered.

"It can be left right here." Mr. Kroop patted the principal's desk. "Or with the secretary. No questions asked."

Winston couldn't speak. He felt as if the ground was slipping from beneath him.

"Away you go then," Mr. Kroop sat up sharply, his voice harsh once more. "This won't be the end of it. That money will be found. And if it isn't here soon, whoever took it will be punished severely. Now go back to your classroom."

Winston slouched out of the office and down the stairs to the boys' washroom. Entering a cubicle, he locked the door and, feeling miserable and confused, slumped onto the toilet seat.

Ideas swam wildly in his mind. How could Mr. Kroop say I took the money? Mrs. Whitestar must've told him about me being in early. But yesterday she was there first. I should've told him that. Why would she lie? I thought she liked me. Does she think I took it? She probably told the whole class why I was sent to the office.

Chapter 24

A FEW MINUTES AFTER THE RECESS BELL RANG, the intruder walked along the empty hall. A classroom door was unlocked and opened, closed and then relocked from the inside.

The intruder crouched beside a desk. Books were pulled out and placed on the seat. Two twenty-dollar bills were taken from a pocket, wadded together, tucked behind pieces of crumpled papers at the back of the desk. The books were replaced.

Smiling, the intruder walked to the door, opened and relocked it, and stepped into the hallway.

Chapter 25

WINSTON OPENED THE CUBICLE, LEFT THE washroom, and dragged himself along the basement corridor. Once outside, he shuffled right across the playground and dropped down without turning around. His nose almost touched the wires of the fence.

Before long, he felt someone's leg pressing gently against his back.

"Where were you?" Caroline asked.

"In the office, and then in the washroom."

"What happened?"

"They think I took the money."

"Who? What money?"

"The T-shirt money. Mr. Kroop and Mrs. Whitestar think I stole it."

"Who said that?" Caroline asked, sitting down beside her friend.

"Mr. Kroop. That's why he called me down to the office. He says I stole the money before

Mrs. Whitestar got there yesterday morning."

"That's stupid! Were you even up there yesterday morning?"

"Yes."

"Before Mrs. Whitestar got there?"

"No. But he knows that sometimes I get there before she does."

"Did you tell him that?"

He nodded.

"Winston! Why did you tell him?"

"I couldn't help it! I didn't know he thought I stole the money. First I thought he knew it was me in the school last night. And then I thought he was just bawling me out for breaking his rule about not being in school before the bell. He didn't say anything about the money until I said I get there early sometimes."

"That's really sleazy of him!"

"What about Mrs. Whitestar? She must think I did it too. Or she's just blaming me so she doesn't have to pay."

"I don't think so. She was acting pretty worried when you were gone so long. She even sent Donny to look for you."

"I heard him come into the washroom. I just put my feet up so he couldn't see me."

"I think she felt bad that you never came back."

"She should. She got me into a lot of trouble."

From across the schoolyard came the sound of the bell. Caroline got up and brushed off the back of her jeans. Winston didn't budge.

"Aren't you going to come?"

"No. Everybody must think I stole the money. They probably hate me."

"No one else knows about it. Mrs. Whitestar never said why you went down to the office. And Mr. Kroop wouldn't be dumb enough to say anything. He doesn't have any proof." She held her hand down to him. "Come on."

Winston pushed himself up. "All right. But I might not stay."

Back in the classroom, Winston sat with a hand above his eyes so that all he could see was his desk top. No one was talking about the stolen money or about him going to the office. But even without looking, he was sure everyone was staring at him. He felt hot and angry.

It seemed to take hours for lunchtime to arrive. When it did, Winston quickly left the room. He met the grade eight class coming back from the library.

"Hi, Winston." It was Melody.

Winston murmured something in reply, but didn't slow down.

"Winston, wait." Melody stepped over to his side of the stairs. "Does Caroline still have that lighter?"

"I guess so." Winston tried to get past Melody. "I have to go."

"She should give it to me," Melody said. "I think it's one my friend had stolen. I said I'd help her get it back. Can you get it from Caroline for me."

"Why don't you ask her yourself?" Winston sounded grumpy.

"She wouldn't give it to me, remember?" Melody said. She tipped her head slightly, flicked loose strands of hair off her shoulder, and gave Winston a sad look. "You're always so nice, I thought you'd ask her for me," she said. "She'd give it to you."

"I'll ask her," Winston mumbled.

"Thanks!" Melody smiled broadly. "My friend's worried about it because it's worth a lot. I don't know how it ended up in your room."

"Whatever."

"See you later!" Melody slipped into a bunch of grade eights climbing the stairs.

Walking with his head down, Winston was shocked by the bump that threw him into the wall. He looked over to see Kelvin and another boy laughing at him.

"Watch where you're going, Wilson," Kelvin said. "You could get into trouble hitting people like that."

"Watch out yourself," Winston muttered.

"Careful, Wilson, those are fighting words." Kelvin held his fists in front of his chest and pretended to jab at Winston's face.

"Come on, Kelvin," the other boy said. "I want to get going."

"Sure. Take it easy, Wilson." Kelvin tapped Winston's shoulder as he walked past.

Winston groaned. Everyone around here, he said to himself, thinks they can boss me around.

Through the doorway to Mrs. Whitestar's room, Melody saw Mr. Kroop approach the teacher's desk.

"What are you doing here?" Melissa asked from her locker.

"Oh, hi, sis," Melody said. "You going home for lunch?"

"Yes. I suppose you want me to get something for you."

"No," Melody replied, still watching the two teachers. Mr. Kroop was leaning over the desk, toward Mrs. Whitestar. They seemed to be arguing. "I'm going home, too. I thought we could walk together."

"That's a switch. You usually don't want to."

Seeing Melody, Mr. Kroop came back to close the door.

"I wonder what they're up to," Melody said.

"Who cares. I'm hungry. Let's go."

"Go in and find out what they're talking about."

"What?" Melissa said. "No way. You go, if you're so interested."

"I can't. It's your room. Say you forgot something in your desk."

"I don't want to."

"Mell-iss-ssa." Melody drew out each syllable, her jaw tightening. "Now."

Melissa threw her backpack onto the floor and glared at her sister. She opened the door, closed it partly, and was gone for less than a minute. When she returned, she picked up her pack and stuffed in a book. Without speaking, Melissa started down the stairs. Melody hurried after her.

"So?" Melody asked.

"Mrs. Whitestar was mad. Mr. Kroop kept saying he had to do it. She said she didn't want him to, because she trusted her students. He said he was going to do it in every room."

"Do what?"

"Search desks for the missing money."

"It's about time," Melody said.

Chapter 26

PULLING HIS SPOON BACK AND FORTH ACROSS THE bowl, Winston was making tiny red waves in his tomato soup. The bowl was almost full, the soup cold and thickening on top. His phone rang.

"Hi, Winston," Caroline said, "How're you feeling?"

"*Betrayed. Got into trouble by someone you thought was your friend.*"

"Sorry. I was wondering if we could talk before the end of lunch recess."

"About what?" Winston asked.

"About Henry and Mr. Z. We still have to tell Mrs. Whitestar where they are."

"I'm not going to tell her anything," Winston said. "I hate her."

"Winston! She didn't do anything. It was Mr. Kroop who said you stole the money."

"Yes, but she must have told him I did it.

102

Anyway, those guinea pigs are okay. They've got lots of food and water."

Caroline was silent for a moment. "You're right," she said. "I shouldn't be worrying about them any more. We don't know who took them, but at least we know they're safe. And now we really have to find out who stole the money. Let's talk about that instead. Will we meet at the usual place?"

"I'm not going back to school. I don't want to sit in that classroom when everyone thinks I took the money."

"You're going to stay home?" Caroline asked. "Is your mom there?"

"She's here now. She's going to work."

"Are you going to tell her?"

"No. I'll just say I'm sick."

"I wish you were going to be there," Caroline said. "We have lots to do. Come to my place later."

Winston didn't answer.

"After school, I'm going to Heather's so we can finish our science report. She lives over by the river. I'll get back about 4:30. Come then, okay?"

There was still no response from Winston.

"Mom made something you really like last night," Caroline said. "Chocolate puffed wheat cake. We can have some when you get here, all right?"

"Maybe," Winston mumbled.

Chapter 27

ENRY'S CLAWS CAUGHT ON THE CARDBOARD BOX. He pulled, but the claws wouldn't let go. He pulled again, and again, until the strip ripped off the side. Henry gnawed at the cardboard and soon lifted his paw free.

After raising his snout to sniff the lettuce and carrots, Henry shuffled into the hole. Gripping the floorboards, he pried himself through. With many stops to test the air, the guinea pig plodded around the corner of the box. Grabbing the leaf of lettuce in his paws, he began to nibble.

Back in the box, Mr. Z slept.

Chapter 28

CAROLINE WAS READING WHEN HER TEACHER CALLED to her. She walked to Mrs. Whitestar's desk. "I'm just wondering about Winston," Mrs. Whitestar began. "I got a message that he was home sick this afternoon. Do you know if he wasn't feeling well?"

"Sort of."

"Hmmm." Mrs. Whitestar narrowed her eyes as she looked closely at Caroline. When she spoke again, she was whispering. "I want you to tell me the truth now. Is he feeling bad about..." she paused, "something that happened at school?"

Caroline looked down. "Yes."

"Can you tell me about it?"

"He's really mad at Mr. Kroop." Caroline peeked at her teacher. "And you."

Mrs. Whitestar's forehead wrinkled. "Me?" she asked.

"Yes," Caroline said. "He told me that Mr. Kroop said he thought Winston stole the T-shirt money. And that you must have told Mr. Kroop that he did it."

"When did this happen?" Mrs. Whitestar asked. "When he was at the office this morning?"

Caroline nodded.

"I said no such thing!" Mrs. Whitestar's voice rose. The children sitting close by looked toward her. She leaned closer to Caroline to whisper again. "That's terrible! I'd never think Winston is a thief." Mrs. Whitestar raised one hand to rub her forehead. "He thinks that I think he stole the money? I'll have to phone him at recess." She sighed. "And then I guess I'll have to go talk to Mr. Kroop. Mrs. B. is coming back tomorrow. Maybe she can sort all this out."

Shortly after, the recess bell rang. Caroline stayed seated, staring at the pages of her book. When everyone else had left the room, she got up and closed the door. Then she went back to her desk.

In the midst of a daydream about capturing the thief, Caroline was startled by Mr. Kroop.

"What are you doing up here?"

Caroline gasped. She looked toward the door, expecting to see it open and the vice-principal glowering at her. The door was closed.

"I asked what you were doing," Mr. Kroop repeated angrily from the hall.

"Just getting a ball," someone answered.

Who's that? Caroline wondered.

"Well, you've got it, so get going. You're not supposed to be in here at recess."

"Right." *Thum, thum, thum* came the sound of a ball bouncing.

"And stop bouncing that ball, Kelvin, or I'll bounce you – right down the stairs."

Thum. Caroline heard the ball hit the floor once more; a few seconds later, more bounces, this time quieter, from part way down the stairs. She held her breath, hoping Mr. Kroop wouldn't look into her classroom. He didn't.

Chapter 29

IS HUNGER LESSENED, HENRY WALKED AROUND the corner of the box and back through the hole. He shuffled across the paper towels, then lay with his snout resting on his front paws.

Mr. Z stirred in his sleep. He got up and made his way past Henry to the hole. After checking the air outside the box, Mr. Z turned and waddled back to the pile of kibble.

Chapter 30

WHEN THE PHONE RANG, WINSTON DIDN'T WANT to answer it. After eight or nine rings, he wondered if it might be his mother. He picked up the receiver.

"Hel-lo," he said, trying to make his voice sound woozy.

"Hi, Winston. This is Melody."

"Oh, hi."

"Did you get the lighter?"

"I didn't go to school after lunch."

"Well, when are you going to see Caroline?"

"Maybe later."

"Winston, you said you'd get it for me. I'm depending on you. It's a favour for my friend."

"Okay."

"Good. I'll be waiting."

Chapter 31

A COOL WIND SWEPT ACROSS THE WATER. Overhead, the pale blue sky was cloudless. Caroline tugged her jacket further down over her hips and pulled the zipper as high as it would go. From the road on the way to Heather's house, she could see a group of white pelicans swimming below the waterfall. She dashed across the street between cars and followed a path down the hill to the river.

When she got close to the shore, she slowed down and stepped carefully from rock to rock. But before she reached the edge of the water, the two pelicans nearest her rapidly beat their black-tipped wings. The birds lifted into the air, their legs trailing in the water like two long ropes, and flew closer to the waterfall.

Caroline crouched down, hugged her arms around her knees, and for the next few minutes watched the pelicans search for fish.

A rock shot over Caroline's head like a missile and struck the water short of the pelicans. Caroline jumped up – feet skittering on loose stones – and turned clumsily. Kelvin was standing just behind her. Caroline stepped backwards, away from the boy, further up the riverbank.

"Get out of here," Kelvin said. "You're in my way." He bent down to pick up another rock.

"I heard you getting bawled out today by Mr. Kroop," Caroline said.

"So? What of it?"

"Kind of dumb to get in trouble just for a ball."

Kelvin snorted. "That's not why I was up- stairs. Some guys bet me I wouldn't go in when Kroop was there."

"You did it just to get caught by Mr. Kroop?" Caroline asked, sounding as if she didn't believe him.

"Sure. He goes nuts whenever he sees me. And he's nothing to be afraid of. He's like one of those yappy little dogs – all bark and no bite. Kroop just thinks he's big when Mrs. Bobowski's not there. But she's the boss."

"She's coming back tomorrow," Caroline said. "Then what'll you do?"

"Keep my nose clean, for one thing," Kelvin said. "I don't mess with Mrs. B. She's one tough lady."

111

"Mrs. Bobowski? I think she's really nice."

"For someone like you, she's nice." The way Kelvin said it, nice wasn't something he wanted to be. "For someone like me, she's tough. If you do anything, you pay for it. She's fair, though, and not mean. Just tough."

"Hey," Caroline whispered. "Look what they're doing."

Kelvin turned to face the river. Near them, a fast stream of water shot around the end of the weir from top to bottom. As they watched, a single pelican came speeding down the stream and out into the waves at the bottom of the waterfall.

A second pelican paddled to the top of the weir. Just as it was being sucked into the racing water, the bird hiked its folded wings further up on its back. More pelicans splashed down above the weir, forming a line to take turns riding down the chute.

The first two birds had let themselves be carried further down the river. As they drifted past, the pelicans stared with unblinking eyes at the children.

"Wow!" Caroline exclaimed softly. "What beautiful birds. And they're so big."

"Big money for me if one ever gets close."

"What do you mean?"

Kelvin smiled. "My uncle will pay me good for one of those suckers. He stuffs them."

"That's gross!"

"What's gross? They shoot ducks, don't they? And geese. And stuff them. And deer and foxes and all kinds of other animals." He tossed the rock lightly in his hand. "One less pelican won't make any difference."

Before he could throw the stone, Caroline asked, "Do you know whose this is?" Holding her hand near her side, she opened her palm to show the silver lighter.

Kelvin's eyes flashed on the lighter. Dropping the rock, his arm darted toward Caroline. "I could use that," he said.

Caroline stepped backwards and turned sideways. The lighter slipped into her jeans pocket.

"Let me see that," Kelvin snarled. He opened his hand and curled his fingers in and out.

Caroline dodged to the side and took off. "You chase me and I'll scream," she cried over her shoulder. Then she was racing up the path toward the road and Heather's house.

Chapter 32

NOT LONG AFTER SHE GOT TO HER HOUSE, Caroline opened the front door for her friend.

"You still mad?" she asked, looking at Winston's frown.

"What do you think?" Winston said, heading for the kitchen table. "How would you like to be accused of stealing?"

When they sat down, the yellow cat strolled out from beside the fridge and rubbed against Winston's leg.

"Get away!" he said crossly. He pushed the cat with his foot. "What's he doing in here?" he asked. "I thought you weren't going to keep him."

"We're not," Caroline said. "This is his last day."

As she spoke, the cat stepped into Grannie's basket and lay against the dog's bulk.

Caroline opened a plastic container and offered Winston some cake. He took two pieces. Like a giant turtle peering from her shell, Grannie poked her head out from under the bottom of the table cloth.

"Forget it," Winston said.

The sad eyes silently slipped out of sight. In a moment the dog's front legs stuck out from the basket. After sliding them into a long stretch, she hauled the rest of her body out from under the table.

"It walks!" Winston said.

The dog sat on her haunches, her eyes level with Caroline's chest. Whining softly, Grannie pulled one paw across Caroline's lap. Her eyes darted quickly from Caroline's face to the cake in her hand and back.

"I know you like chocolate," Caroline said, "but you can't have any of this. It sticks to your gums." To Winston she added, "Mom says if I give her stuff like this, I have to brush her teeth."

"Yuck," Winston said.

Caroline slid the container of cake closer to him. "Have more," she said. "Want some juice?"

With his mouth full, Winston nodded yes.

As she filled two glasses, Caroline said, "Mrs. Whitestar told me she was going to phone you. What did she say?"

"Not much. Mostly that she was sorry. She said Mr. Kroop asked her who comes upstairs before the bell rings, because they might have seen something. She told him I do sometimes, but she never said I might've taken the money."

"Don't you believe her?"

"I guess so," Winston said.

Grannie pawed at Caroline's lap. "All gone," she said. The dog barked once, then, tail drooping on the floor, slouched under the table. Grannie stopped, whimpered, and backed up a step.

Winston pulled up the tablecloth. In the centre of the basket, the cat was stretched out on his side. He blinked lazily and his claws slipped out and in as he gazed at the dog.

Grannie's front paws clacked a brittle tap dance on the floor. She barked and stepped close enough that her head reached over the basket.

In an instant, the cat was on his feet. Like a little boxer, he poked one paw, with the claws out, at the dog's nose. Grannie backed up and whined. She looked at Caroline, then lay down in front of her.

"Oh, Grannie." Caroline shook her head. "You are such a wimp." She reached down to pet the cat, then pulled him into her arms. "And you," she said, "are really wearing out your welcome."

Caroline took the cat outside. As she bent down and opened her arms, the cat leaped to the sidewalk. Turning to face Caroline, he lifted up a front paw to lick his fur. "You'd better leave while you can," she said. "You won't want to be around when my mom gets home."

Under the kitchen table, Grannie happily padded down her cushion.

That cat, Winston thought, reminds me of another bully. He saw again the video that had been replaying in his mind all afternoon. In it, Kelvin was smiling and pinching his shoulder. Then the picture changed and Kelvin was standing beside the janitor's cart, holding a ring of keys and a wastebasket. The picture changed again and Kelvin was laughing and pretending to punch his arm. "I'm not looking for trouble," Kelvin was saying. "You can even keep your money today." Kelvin didn't rob him that last time, Winston had figured out, because he'd just stolen the T-shirt money.

Winston was ready when Caroline sat back down beside him. "I've been thinking," he said. "Kelvin's been helping Mr. Janzen all week. He could've taken Henry and Mr. Z while he was cleaning our room. And he had Mr. Janzen's keys. So if the janitor's room was locked he could get in and hide them in that old storeroom. Then, the next day, he could've taken the money."

Caroline instantly agreed with him. "Winston, you're brilliant!" she exclaimed. "I've been trying to find more clues and you just sat there and figured it out."

Winston shrugged.

"The same person did both. Of course!" Caroline said. She reached down to unzip the top of her backpack. "Now we just have to figure out who that person was."

"I just told you who it was," Winston said, sounding annoyed.

Ignoring Winston's words, Caroline plonked a pencil and a piece of paper on the table in front of him. "We'll write down everything we know about both thefts," she said. "And put them together. That's like having twice as many clues to catch just one person. So..." she looked at Winston. "You write first, okay?"

Then she continued. "Keys – who can get keys for the rooms? Hiding place for Henry and Mr. Z – who would know about that secret door? And that lighter – who smokes? And who's missing a lighter? If the same person answers all of these questions, for sure we've got the thief!"

Winston let the video play once more in his head. He knew who the culprit was. But he also knew that the image forming in Caroline's head was going to be a different person altogether. Frowning, he slapped at the wisp of hair floating beside his head.

Chapter 33

AS IF HE KNEW THE DAY WAS ALMOST OVER, HENRY roused himself from his nap. Dropping his snout into the jar lid, he splashed some water into his mouth with his tongue. He raised and jiggled his head to swallow. Shuffling to the hole in the box, Henry pushed through the opening and lay down to nibble on a carrot.

Mr. Z opened his eyes and lumbered over to the hole. He poked his nose through to the other side, and sniffed. Then he squeezed further into the opening until, about half-way through, his body rubbed snugly against the cardboard on all sides. Mr. Z laid his head on the floor and closed his eyes.

FRIDAY

Chapter 34

THE LAYERS OF DIRT SMUDGING THE WINDOWS HIGH above the little room were like curtains that blocked out the strong morning sun. In an open space beside the cardboard box, a guinea pig held a shred of lettuce in his two front paws. Henry pulled his paws closer to munch on the moist leaf.

Hidden in the shadows of a nearby jumble of ski boots, Mr. Z slept. He hadn't moved since the afternoon before when he'd finally tracked down the carrot.

Chapter 35

CAROLINE PACED BACK AND FORTH OUTSIDE THE entrance door. Nearby, Winston stood with his back against the school. The sun had climbed above the treetops and Winston, motionless and eyes closed, was a cat being warmed by the rays.

When he heard Caroline come near, Winston asked, "So, how's Grannie doing with that stray?"

"He's gone," Caroline said.

Winston opened his eyes. "Where?"

"I don't know," Caroline said. "We haven't seen him since I put him outside yesterday. He must have got mad and left."

"Gone to mooch off somebody else," Winston said, closing his eyes again.

"I guess. I hope he finds a home somewhere. Mom was getting tired of him, so he wouldn't have lasted much longer anyway."

Through a window in the door, a teacher peered out at the children in the playground. He held his hand up to his forehead to shield his eyes from the sun's glare, and sipped coffee from his cup.

"He should let us in," Caroline said. "Mrs. Bobowski's in there, probably talking about the thefts, and we know who did it. We have to talk to her before she gets the wrong person."

"Did you tell him that?" Winston nodded toward the teacher's face showing through the window.

"He won't listen. We can't go in until the bell goes."

When they reached the principal's office, Caroline and Winston found the school secretary talking on the telephone. The moment Mrs. Leedahl put down the receiver, Caroline said, "We have to see Mrs. Bobowski. It's really important."

"Mrs. Bobowski is busy," Mrs. Leedahl said, glancing at the closed door beside her desk. "She has people with her. You'll have to come back later." The phone rang. The secretary answered it and pulled another piece of paper from a pile in front of her.

Caroline and Winston walked a few steps further down the hall to a second door to the principal's office. Through a window in that door, they could see three people. Mrs. Bobowski was behind the desk, forehead wrinkled, mouth firmly set, plump arms resting on the desktop. Mr. Kroop perched on a chair near one corner of the principal's desk, his eyes gleaming and his face flushed. Across from him, Kelvin kicked at a spot on the carpet.

"We're too late!" Caroline exclaimed. She walked closer to the door.

Seeing the movement, all three people inside the office glanced toward her. Mr. Kroop said something, but not loud enough for Caroline to hear. Kelvin looked down at the principal's desk. Mrs. Bobowski waved her hand to tell Caroline and Winston to leave.

"We have to do something," Caroline said.

"Not right now." Winston took a step backward. "Mrs. Bobowski doesn't look like she wants to be disturbed."

"If she finds out everything, she won't be mad at us," Caroline said. "I'm going to tell her."

Caroline walked up to the door. Keeping her eye on Mrs. Bobowski, she knocked. The principal shook her head hard enough to ruffle her thick silvery-blonde hair. When Mrs. Bobowski turned to Mr. Kroop, Caroline knocked a third time.

Mr. Kroop glared at Caroline. He started to get up from his chair. Caroline saw Mrs. Bobowski say something to the vice-principal, who sat back down. Mrs. Bobowski got up, walked to the door, and opened it.

"Caroline," the principal said, "whatever it is, it has to wait. You mustn't interrupt. We're dealing with a very serious matter right now. If you must see me, you can come back at recess."

"It can't wait," Caroline said. Seeing Mrs. Bobowski was getting angry, Caroline kept on. "It's about..." she lowered her voice, "it's about the thefts. The money and the guinea pigs. We know who did it."

"Now, Caroline..." Mrs. Bobowski began.

"It wasn't Kelvin. We found a clue that proves who really did it." Caroline opened her hand to show the lighter.

After a glimpse at the silver tube, Mrs. Bobowski pointed to the wall across from her office. "Stay there for now," she said.

Turning back to Winston, Caroline heard Mrs. Bobowski tell Mr. Kroop to take Kelvin to his classroom. Frowning, and herding Kelvin in front of him like a prisoner, the vice-principal left the office. Mrs. Bobowski waved to Caroline and Winston and had them sit in the chairs in front of his desk.

"I repeat," Mrs. Bobowski said, as she closed the door behind them, "this is a very serious matter." She walked to her chair. "So, what do you two have to say?"

Chapter 36

FIVE MINUTES LATER, MRS. BOBOWSKI OPENED the door for Caroline and Winston to leave.

"I guess you'd better stick around," the principal said. "There are some chairs by Mrs. Leedahl's desk. Ask her to let Mrs. Whitestar know where you are." Mrs. Bobowski closed the door to her office, picked up the phone and dialed.

It didn't seem very long before Caroline and Winston heard heavy breathing and hurried footsteps approaching down the hallway. Melody's and Melissa's mother, with an angry look on her face, marched past Mrs. Leedahl. Without knocking, she opened Mrs. Bobowski's door and closed it heavily behind her.

The wall between the two rooms wasn't thick enough to hide the sound of shouting coming from the principal's office. When the shouting switched to loud crying, Caroline bit her lip.

Winston raised his eyebrows. "*Humiliation*," he said. "*Having your pride hurt. And everyone knowing it.*" Caroline nodded.

In a short while, the loud noises stopped. Mrs. Leedahl's phone rang. "Yes, Mrs. Bobowski," she said. The secretary pushed a button on the intercom system. "Mr. Kroop," she said, "please bring Melody to the office."

The sounds of shouting and crying again pierced the wall. Mrs. Leedahl asked Caroline and Winston to go to the back of her office and staple together some booklets of scrap paper.

Melody's mother burst into the hall. "Melody will be at home for the rest of the day," she said. "I have to go to work. I swear I don't know what to do. Her father will deal with her when he gets home." Her hand tightly gripping her daughter's elbow, she spat out, "You are a disgrace to your family." Melody stared at the floor in front of her.

When he came out of the office, Mr. Kroop's face was a deep purple. Tugging his tie wildly from side to side, the vice-principal hurried off down the corridor.

"Mr. Kroop!" Mrs. Leedahl called. When he turned, she held out her hand toward him. "Is this yours?"

From where they were standing, Caroline

and Winston saw a flash of silver in the secretary's hand.

Caroline gaped. "Is that the lighter?" she whispered.

"Yes," Mr. Kroop said, returning to the office. "That is mine. Where was it? Who had it?"

Winston slipped closer to the secretary's desk. "Mrs. Bobowski gave it to me," Mrs. Leedhal said. "She found it in her desk drawer. She thought you might have left it there."

"Mmph!" Mr. Kroop muttered, grabbing the silvery object and spinning around to head back down the hall.

Winston looked back at Caroline and shrugged. "It was just a teacher's chalk holder," he said. "Nothing special."

Mrs Bobowski came to the secretary's desk. "I'll be busy awhile longer," she said. "Caroline, Winston, come back in please."

Chapter 37

WHEN THEY WERE ALL SEATED, MRS. BOBOWSKI breathed out deeply. "Well," she said, "it seems you were right. Why don't you tell me how you did it."

"Sure," Caroline said. "When Henry and Mr. Z were taken, we found the lighter right away and that gave us a clue. But we couldn't think why someone would take two guinea pigs. And then when the money was stolen we could guess why – somebody was really greedy. We just didn't have any clues about who it might be. For a long time we were stuck, trying to solve two crimes and not having any luck with either one. Then yesterday–"

"I was home because I was sick," Winston butted in, "and I got thinking that it could be the same person who did both. So when Caroline came over after school–"

"We made a list," Caroline took over, "of everything we knew. And who the likely suspects were."

"When we finished the list," Winston said, "there were only two people who could have done it. Kelvin and Melody."

"They both could get keys," Caroline said, "and they both probably knew about the secret storeroom. But we decided it was Melody. Because she told Winston once that she didn't know how the lighter got in our room. And we never told anyone that's where we found it."

"Then yesterday," Winston added, "she kept bugging me to get it back."

"And well she should have," Mrs. Bobowski said. "The lighter is some keepsake of her mother's. Melody had taken it without permission, to show off to her friends, I guess. Then lost it. Melody knew that her mother had already phoned the school to have us watch out for the lighter. So she knew that if it turned up in your room, I'd know whose it was. And she'd be linked with the missing money. Which is exactly what happened."

Leaning back, hands clasped behind her head, Mrs Bobowski continued. "I think that's why she stole the money, too. Just to show off. To prove how smart she was. Did you know that she took the money at the same time as the guinea pigs?"

Winston and Caroline shook their heads "no."

"She had this fancy plan," Mrs. Bobowski

said. "I don't know where she got the idea, on television maybe. She took the guinea pigs and then put that stuff in a locker just so people wouldn't notice the missing money. Then, the next day, when Mrs. Whitestar would find the money gone, Melody stayed home – so no one would even think of her. She can be a very devious young lady."

"*Devious. Being dishonest*," Winston said. "*And sneaky.*"

"I know," Caroline said. "Don't interrupt Mrs. Bobowski."

The principal went on. "She figured all she had to do was connect the money to Kelvin, who's always getting into trouble anyway. And Mr. Kroop would blame him for the theft.

"And she just about succeeded. Last night Mr. Kroop found some money Melody had put in Kelvin's desk. That convinced him Kelvin was the thief. I admit I was convinced too. I was about to lower the boom on him when you came along this morning."

"He said you were tough," Caroline said.

"Kelvin said that?" Mrs. Bobowski asked. She chuckled. "He's right, too. He and I have an understanding. When he's at school, he has to follow the rules."

Mrs. Bobowski picked up a pencil and lightly tapped it on her desk. She looked over at Caroline and Winston.

"Kelvin has a hard time at school," she said, "because he comes here angry a lot." She paused again. "This is just for the three of us to know, but his home isn't always a very happy place. Sometimes his mom kind of gives up and he has to take care of himself. There have been days when there wasn't even any food in the house."

"What happens then?" Caroline asked.

"Sometimes we can help him out," Mrs. Bobowski said. "Other times he seems to find a way to get money to buy food himself."

"He still shouldn't pick on people," Winston said.

"I agree," Mrs. Bobowski said. "He can't use that as an excuse for being a bully, which is how he sometimes acts."

"Can we get the guinea pigs now?" Caroline blurted.

"Ah, yes!" Mrs. Bobowski exclaimed, "the guinea pigs. You haven't told me how you found the guinea pigs."

"Caroline figured that one out by herself," Winston said. "She thought of the one place where no one else had looked."

"But Winston's the hero," Caroline said. "He was the brave one that night. We almost got caught and then I got scared in the dark and–"

"Wait!" Mrs Bobowski threw up her hands. "I don't think I want to hear this. Does it have anything to do with a nighttime visit to our school?"

Caroline and Winston nodded.

"I'm right. I don't want to hear about it. That does clear up one more mystery though. And yes," she said brightly, "we can go get the guinea pigs. First, we'd better fill Mrs. Whitestar in. I'll tell you what. You two go back to your room and tell your teacher how you solved all this. Then bring her and meet me at the janitor's supply room."

Mrs. Bobowski pushed herself up from her desk. "It'll take me a few minutes to get there. I have a couple of things to do here first. And then I'm going to talk to someone on the way."

Chapter 38

IN THE HALLWAY OUTSIDE THEIR CLASSROOM, Caroline and Winston retold their story for their teacher.

"You mean you did all this by yourselves?" Mrs. Whitestar asked when they had finished. "Why didn't you ever tell me anything? You didn't even tell me about that lighter."

"At first," Caroline said, "I guess we wanted to do it ourselves and then surprise you, and then...." Seeing Winston scowling and looking like he didn't want to talk about it, Caroline stopped.

"Okay," Mrs. Whitestar said, "I know the rest." She spoke to Winston. "And then I got you into trouble without even knowing I had. And you probably didn't want to talk to me, period. I'm really sorry about that, Winston. I hope that never happens again."

"It's all right," Winston mumbled. "I know it wasn't your fault."

Mrs. Whitestar reached out to give Winston a quick hug. "And how did you know where Henry and Mr. Z were?" she asked.

As Caroline answered, Winston saw Mrs. Bobowski come up the stairs at the far end of the hall. She knocked on the door to the grade eight classroom. When Kelvin came out, he slumped against the wall and faced Mrs. Bobowski as she stood with her hands on her hips.

A few moments later, the principal nodded toward Caroline, Winston, and Mrs. Whitestar. Kelvin twisted part way around. To Winston, it looked as though Kelvin sneered in his direction before saying something to Mrs. Bobowski. Winston glowered at Kelvin's back.

Melissa strode through the doorway. She saw Mrs. Bobowski, then spoke to Mrs. Whitestar in a loud voice. "No one's working in there. And Donny's throwing things around the room. I've told them to stop, but they won't listen." She turned to Caroline and Winston, "Are you two in trouble?"

"Melissa," Mrs. Whitestar said, "don't be such a busybody. I'll talk to the kids, but then I'm going to be gone for awhile." She grasped Melissa's arm and went back into the classroom.

"I saw you staring at Kelvin," Caroline said to Winston. "You really hate him, don't you?"

"He's an *evildoer*," he said. "*Someone who....*" he paused. "You know what it means. And I bet he doesn't even thank us for getting him off."

"Maybe not," Caroline said. "But we still know we did it. And so does Mrs. Whitestar. What did he ever do to you anyway?"

Before Winston had to answer, their teacher joined them. "Let's go," she said. "Here comes Mrs. Bobowski." She looked at Winston. "Hey, cheer up," she said. "You're the heroes, remember."

The principal opened the door and let Caroline, Winston, and Mrs. Whitestar go in the supply room first. Each of the four moved a box from in front of the door to the storeroom. As Caroline was opening that door, Winston spotted Donny sneaking in behind them.

"It's about Henry and Mr Z, right?" he asked. "You found them, right? Are they dead or what?"

Mrs. Whitestar answered first. "Yes," she said, "it's about Henry and Mr. Z. And, yes, you may come along. But watch only, no more talking."

Winston punched on the light and led Mrs. Bobowski and the others single file past the piles of dusty boxes. Opening the door to the little room, he exclaimed, "Ta daaa! Two guinea pigs!"

Mrs. Bobowski stepped into the room. "Well, good for–" she stopped. "Winston, there aren't two guinea pigs here, there's only one!"

"What!" Winston gasped.

Caroline shouldered past the principal. Looking up at her from the bottom of the box was one long-haired butterscotch-coloured guinea pig. "Henry!" she said, bending down to pick him up.

"What's going on?" Mrs. Whitestar asked, trapped at the end of the line behind Donny and between two stacks of boxes.

Winston squeezed by Mrs. Bobowski on the other side. "Look," he said. "There's a hole. Mr. Z got out." Frantically he poked at the boxes and skiis. "He's probably lost!"

"He's not lost," Donny said.

The others turned to look at Donny. Cupped close to his chest was the short-haired, creamy-white and spotted guinea pig.

"He was right here beside this box," Donny said. "You guys walked right by him."

"Mr. Z!" Winston was laughing, but almost crying with relief. "You are the smartest! That's what I kept telling Caroline."

"What do you mean?" Mrs. Whitestar asked.

"Caroline wouldn't believe that Mr. Z was smarter than Henry," Winston explained. "She thought he was just lazy. But if Mr. Z got all the way over there," he pointed to Donny, "he was the one who made the hole. Henry has been sitting in the box waiting to be rescued."

"Is that true, Henry?" Caroline asked, ruffling the fur on the guinea pig's back.

Henry lifted his nose to sniff and peer around him.

Lying in Donny's palm, Mr. Z closed his eyes and seemed to smile as he tucked his two front paws under the tip of his snout.

Dave Glaze has spent almost twenty years in the field of education as a teacher, teacher-librarian, and consultant. He has written for and edited magazines, newspapers, and the publications of a number of community-based organizations.

His first novel for young readers, *Pelly* (Coteau Books), was honoured with the Children's Choice Award from the Canadian Children's Book Centre in 1993.

Glaze is currently an elementary schoolteacher and librarian. He lives in Saskatoon, Saskatchewan, with his wife and two daughters.

About the illustrator:

Janet Wilson is a freelance illustrator whose work has appeared in magazines, advertisements, books, and films. She most enjoys producing children's picture books and has received international acclaim for such works as *Daniel's Dog, How to be Cool in the Third Grade,* and *In Flanders Field.*

Wilson is an honours graduate of the Ontario College of Art. She lives and works in Eden Mills, Ontario, with her husband, broadcaster Chris Wilson. They have two sons.